me and the cute catastrophe

catastrophe

Sweet, Small Town Romantic Comedy in Good Grief, Idaho

Book One

jessie gussman

contents

acknowledgments

Cover art by Julia Gussman
Editing by Heather Hayden
Narration by Jay Dyess
Author Services by CE Author Assistant

———

Listen to the unabridged audio for FREE performed by Jay Dyess on the Say with Jay channel on YouTube. Get early access to all of Jay's recordings and listen to Jessie's books before they're available to the general public, plus get daily Bible readings by Jay and bonus scenes by becoming a Say with Jay channel member.

one

. . .

Claire

I WAS GOING to start this book out with a nice introduction of myself and tell you that my name is Claire Harding and I'm a home nurse, divorced with two girls, and my ex is a jerk.

But my plans got interrupted a little, and I'm currently scrunched down behind my car, the bumper digging into my back, my daughter's —extremely heavy—pink unicorn bookbag clutched to my chest, and I am praying—because I do pray and not just when I'm in trouble—that my sister will not answer the door, and Trey Haywood will walk back over to his father's house or, better yet, get in his car and drive back to Washington where he belongs.

God answers prayers. I know He does. I've seen it. But he doesn't answer this one.

And I just want to be clear, I don't usually do this. I am forty-one years old, and typically I don't hide from people.

But my daughter Melody, who's ten, is cooking supper. (*Lord, please don't let the kitchen catch on fire. At least not until Trey leaves.*)

I know all of you are probably thinking I'm afraid my homeowner's insurance isn't up-to-date. The real fear though, if the house catches on fire, is that my mom will show up.

She's the fire chief in Good Grief, the town in which I live. It's a volunteer company. Mom goes to every fire.

I don't know about all of you, but I love my mom. I do. Still, I definitely don't want her to show up now. Not when Trey is here.

Anyway, my daughter Melody, she's exactly like me and has trouble getting her nose out of a book long enough to breathe, is cooking supper, so I told her I would get her bookbag.

And yes, she's in fifth grade and way too old for a pink unicorn bookbag, but she's the kind of girl who totally doesn't pay attention to that kind of thing and would still be using the bookbag she used in kindergarten if it hadn't fallen apart.

She gets attached to stuff just like I do.

Stuff like her father.

That was all my fault. If I hadn't gotten old and ugly, he wouldn't have left.

Anyway, that has nothing to do with me and what I'm doing right now, crouched behind my car.

Like I said, I don't normally do this, but I was in the middle of dyeing my hair. Yeah, for those of you who haven't been cursed with the early gray—I got it from my dad—it stinks.

If I didn't dye it, I'd be almost completely gray, and I've been tempted to let it go. After all, I only started hiding the gray to begin with because my husband didn't want to be married to someone who looked like she was older than he was. Now that he's been gone— goodness, has it been eight years already?—I don't need to stay young-looking for him.

I guess I just didn't want to give him the satisfaction of seeing me and thinking how old I looked and how glad he wasn't with me.

Clutching the bag to my chest, I shake those thoughts out of my head. I can't think about Cody without feeling like a loser.

He would be the first person to say I actually *was* a loser. There are so many times I think he's right.

I close my eyes and lean my head against the back of my car.

I suppose I'm some kind of loser to be sitting hunched down behind my car hoping my neighbor leaves.

My good-looking, athletic, high-school-crush neighbor.

Please let him go. Please let him go, I chant in my head. A prayer, sure, but one I know I shouldn't be uttering. I should have just squared my shoulders, forgotten about the fact that my hair looks hideous, and walked regally to my house rather than closing the car door quietly, scrunching down, and duck-walking to the back.

It feels like a smack in the forehead when I hear my front door open. My older sister hangs out at my house a lot, and she's as perfect as I am not.

An English teacher.

That's all I need to say about that. Right?

Every word spelled correctly.

Every verb tense perfect.

She can even diagram sentences.

Like I said. She is perfect.

And she did not inherit our dad's propensity for early gray. Her hair is a honey blonde, natural, falling in silky waves to the middle of her back.

She's even older than Trey than I am, but she is perfect for him.

I hear voices mumbling in the background. I'm still trying to dictate how this is going to go down. *Whatever he wants, let it not be me.*

But no such luck on that prayer either.

"Claire! Claire! I know you're out there." That's my sister yelling at me. No-nonsense, like she's still in front of a class of senior high English students who would rather be anywhere else, because who in the world would want to be sitting in high school English when there are frogs in formaldehyde only steps down the hall just waiting to be dissected, right?

More mumbling as they talk in lower tones. I could almost hear my sister saying *she just ran out for her daughter's backpack.* It's not like we have a huge yard or that my car's parked a half an hour away. It's like maybe fifty feet from the house.

There's no way I could have been attacked by a moose or eaten by a grizzly, although we do have both in Idaho.

Not that I've ever seen any.

"Claire." Now my sister sounds exasperated. "I can see your feet underneath the car. What are you doing? Get over here. Trey wants to talk to you."

Man, I hate this. Not only did I do something stupid and immature, now I have to fess up to it.

Resigned, I straighten. But inspiration strikes when my phone, which I'd shoved in the back pocket of my jeans, because yes, I'm old enough to prefer wearing jeans over yoga pants, catches on the bumper of my car and clatters to the ground.

Of course!

I'll just pretend I was on the phone.

My stomach unclenches slightly, and I smile, impressed with my brilliance.

Typically, I'm not the slightest bit creative and am actually quite boring. My ex made sure to tell me that too.

But this is just absolutely a stroke of genius if I do say so myself. Which I have to, because no one else is going to.

Well, possibly my mom, but your parents don't count.

Grabbing my phone, I hold it to my ear with one hand, sliding the pink backpack a little bit to the side with the other. I can block it with my body a little at least so its sparkly brilliance doesn't blind anyone—Trey—as I business walk into the house.

I've got my head down, and I'm nodding and making those humming noises that people make when they're on the phone and agreeing with whoever's talking to them while not interrupting them.

I'm good at that.

Not just on the phone, but as a nurse, I hear a lot of complaints on a daily basis, and while I love what I do and truly enjoy listening to my patients, sometimes you just have to nod and agree, because being sick stinks, and sometimes there's just nothing you can do about it.

Regardless, I've made it to the steps—there's three of them—with Trey and Tammy standing on the stoop.

Figuring I can be a little gracious, I lift my eyes, very, very conscious of the dye that feels like it's solidified in my hair. I typically go for a golden brown, as close to my previous natural shade as possible, but this dye has been in long enough that I'm going to be at least seventeen shades darker than I normally am.

That's fine. I moonlight as the girls' basketball coach, and I can wear a baseball cap, right?

And as a nurse in Idaho, I can wear a beanie, even if it's September. It gets cold early here.

Still, I'm gracious, lifting my fingers in a little wave and putting an expression on my face that says, *goodness, I'd just love to stand here and talk with all of you fun people, but I'm in the middle of a very important phone conversation and just absolutely can't.*

It's a new look for me, but I think I pull it off.

At least judging from the look on Trey's face, he believes me.

The look on my sister's face isn't quite as trusting, but I'm typically not the slightest bit devious. She has her hand on the door, and she pulls it open for me. I might have made it inside and spent the next thirty minutes congratulating myself on my brilliance, except—I hear a phone ring.

Right beside my ear.

It's mine, of course.

two

. . .

Claire

I STOP MID-NOD. Busted. As my (ringing) phone reverberates through the entire town of Good Grief.

Okay. So maybe I'm exaggerating a little. But it feels that way. Definitely Tammy and Trey hear it with no problem.

There have been lots of times in my life where I would really like to have been able to sink through the floor.

This is one of those.

I'm sure that doesn't come as a shock to anyone.

But it also probably doesn't come as a shock to find out that I didn't…sink through the floor, that is.

It's pure fantasy.

Real life doesn't work that way, just in case you're reading this and you're young enough to think that it might.

I can tell you right now. It doesn't.

When you do stupid and embarrassing things, you always have to face the people that you don't want to face and admit the things you don't want to admit. Which makes you feel even more stupid and more embarrassed.

Take it from me.

Although, I'm fresh out of ideas on how to stop doing stupid and embarrassing things. You'll have to get that advice from someone else.

I'm ashamed to say, if my sister hadn't closed the door in front of me, I would have just kept walking.

But I suppose older sisters everywhere have this sense of justice they're born with that keeps them from allowing their younger siblings to get away with anything.

Including pretending to talk on the phone in order to avoid having to face their old high school crush with black blobs of hair dye all around their face and their hair itself looking like someone threw up on it.

Serves me right for going outside, I suppose.

But I was doing a good deed for my daughter. That should count for something. I suppose I'm saying that to the Lord, like He needs me to point it out to him.

I know it doesn't work that way—I do a good deed and get rewarded for it instantly—but it'd be nice if it did.

I stop. The hand holding my phone to my ear drops slowly to my side, and I look at the doorjamb, thinking that I've never pounded that loose nail in. Easier to think about nails than what the next minute or two is going to bring.

I make a mental note to fix it, then gather all of my mental energy and focus on trying not to look as stupid as I feel.

That involves straightening my shoulders and my spine. And I stop trying to hide the sparkly pink unicorn backpack.

I'll be proud of it.

Proud to be holding the sparkly pink thing.

Proud of my marked-up face and gooped-up hair.

Proud of pretending to talk on the phone.

Oh, who am I kidding. I'm not proud of any of it. But I still straighten my back and lift my chin and smile sweetly at my sister.

My phone stops ringing. I didn't even look at it.

Tammy's brows are knotted, and she has that condescending, older sister look on her face. "You remember Trey, don't you, Claire? I mean, I know you do. You had the biggest crush ever on him in high school.

I'm pretty sure you had Trey and Claire in a heart on all of your schoolbooks and possibly even on the walls in your bedroom."

Trey laughs. A deep rumbling laugh that vibrates across my diaphragm as much as I try to not let it touch me.

Can't catch sound waves and pass them to a teammate, as much as I might wish that to be true right now.

"I think you're thinking about Kori, Tammy." Trey's voice, deeper than I remember, is worse than his laugh, and I suck my stomach in, trying to control the weird waves rolling across it.

"No, I'm not."

I suppose it was too much to hope that Tammy would just let it go. I should have known she wouldn't do it until I was writhing on the ground in pain from the acute embarrassment.

She's never quite gotten me to that point, but it's been close.

I have to admit this is one of the worst. Because she's right. I did have a huge crush on Trey. I wrote his name everywhere. His name with my name. His name by itself. His name and our name together with his last name. Didn't everyone do that in high school?

Probably not. Not Tammy, at least. She was too busy diagramming sentences and reading *Hamlet*.

Plus, Trey was so much younger than I was—although he was tall, so he looked older—that I probably really was the only girl in history to have such a huge crush on such a younger kid. In high school at least.

"You and Kori went out, true." Tammy narrows her eyes, and her hand still holds onto the knob, or I would have opened it and gone through.

Maybe I don't have an escape hatch underneath my feet, but there is a door in front of me.

Too bad I couldn't use it without dropping the bookbag I'd gone out to get or putting my phone away, which right now, with the luck I've been having, would end up dropping to the ground.

All right. At this point, I've decided I've been a coward long enough. Yeah, I look hideous, I'm carrying the pink backpack, and I just got busted for pretending to be talking on my phone, but I'm an adult, and I *can* adult.

Even in front of my high school crush.

I allow a little smile to grace my lips, and I look at Tammy, willing my face to have that look that says high school was eons ago, and I barely remember any of it, and I was such a child anyway.

Then I turn my head back to Trey.

This look is a little harder to master, because when his deep blue eyes meet mine, something wild and delicious shoots down the back of my neck, and like it's on springs, it bounces down my legs, hits the ground, and shoots right back up the same path.

It's kind of hard to have a serene, mature expression on one's face when one has zinging bolts of something crazy shooting up and down their back and legs.

But I try.

I'm the stubborn one in the family. The one with bulldog tendencies. It's amazing Tammy has never given me the nickname Bulldog. Not that I would ever suggest it to her, because she would immediately fall in love with that nickname for me and call me Bulldog for the rest of my life.

"Hello, Trey. Of course I remember you. We were neighbors for years."

Tammy snorts, but I ignore her and hope that Trey offers her a tissue.

No such luck. He doesn't even look at her, because his eyes are glued to mine. That's probably because of those bolts of craziness in my body and the laws of attraction and possibly some type of magnet that his body contains that seems to be pulling mine.

I'm going to have to look that one up later this evening. I've never heard of human bodies containing magnets, but I've never had this overwhelming desire to step closer to someone in my life before either.

Not even my ex, whom I did love when we got married and right up until he told me he'd found a twenty-year-old with tight buns and expensive boobs and said he was turning me in.

I probably loved him for a while after that, even though I shouldn't have.

You can't just turn love on and off. I spent a lot of time hoping he'd come back.

Regardless, he didn't.

I don't keep tabs on him; truly, I don't. I deleted my Facebook profile, and I'm not on social media at all, and I have no clue what the guy's doing other than he's supposed to take the girls over summer vacation and he seldom does and never keeps them more than a week or two. Fine with me.

To my knowledge, though, he's still with Expensive Boobs. At least he was the last time he took the girls. I was pretty proud of the fact that when they came back, I didn't even ask if she had a ring on her finger yet.

I took mine off when he served me the divorce papers. I guess after getting those, you don't need to know it's final in order to know it's over.

Still, I didn't pawn them, even though there is a pawnshop in Good Grief.

They are still upstairs in my top dresser drawer, left-hand side, under the fancy underwear that I never wore. Not even when I was married. Definitely not before I was married. I'm not that kind of girl.

I guess the underwear just represents the hope that someday I might be.

I suppose I should have burned them in the backyard the day I hit forty. But I was kinda busy, raising two kids, working a job, and trying to figure out how in the Sam Hill did a person coach a basketball team, that I didn't even think about it.

Someday.

Someday, I'll have a bonfire in the backyard. Burn the underwear that represents youth, and sexiness, and attraction, and seduction, and all those things that I never was and am definitely never going to be.

Maybe, once I do that, I'll get on the Internet long enough to find out if there is underwear for klutzy people. It stands to reason that there should be. Surely there are just as many klutzy people in the world as there are beautiful people.

Surely they need underwear too. Underwear that makes a statement. *Look at me. I'm klutzy.*

Just like the lacy underwear in my drawer says *look at me, I'm sexy.* Except when I put them on, I look stupid.

At least that's what my ex said.

And yeah, by now you're probably wondering why in the world I stayed with him.

I wonder that too sometimes.

When you live in Idaho, though, it's dangerous to wander too far; it's pretty easy to get lost.

At my admission, Tammy smiles a little as though wanting to blurt out that she was sure I more than just "remember" him, but she doesn't, and I keep the mature and slightly superior look on my face. At least I hope that's the way it looks.

I say, "It's been such a long time. High school was so long ago."

He nods. "It was. Although in ways, it feels like yesterday."

"True. Lots of life happened between now and then." I suppose my voice must hold bitterness because his face scrunches minutely.

"I heard you got divorced."

I nod. Then, because that's something I really don't want to talk about, I say, "I heard you got married. Is your wife here with you?" I kind of tilt my head.

I'm pretty sure he's divorced. Two days ago, when the moving van arrived and we didn't know what was happening, Kori, my youngest sister and the one that actually did date him in high school, happened to be here with all of her smiles and energy and endless optimism, and she called Mrs. Thompson who lives on the other side of Trey and his dad and knows everything that goes on in Good Grief.

Kori had the scoop within 10 minutes, and she dished it all to Leah and my mom at the kitchen table while I made cookies with Melody and Tammy pretended to grade papers, but she was listening too.

She's eight years older than Trey, but he's that good.

So yeah, I asked about his wife, but I already am pretty sure she's not with him. She left him, taking their two boys with her.

I find that interesting. When Cody left, he wasn't the slightest bit interested in taking our girls with him.

He hasn't been the slightest bit interested in spending much time with them since he's been gone either.

Expensive Boobs takes up all his time, I guess.

Not that I call her Expensive Boobs in front of the kids. Well, once I slipped up. The first Christmas after he left when he didn't even call. I try hard not to say anything unkind about the ex in front of the kids, but how can you not when they're crying and asking where he was, and they're already upset because it was their first family Christmas where their family wasn't together?

Maybe I'm the only person in the world whose heart feels like a dumpster fire in her chest when her children cry and hurt and I can't do anything about it.

I'm kind of thinking not.

Anyway, I'm so over him.

I was also over Trey before I married Cody. And I'm still over Trey.

This whole magnet, crazy-waves-in-my-chest thing is just weird.

Although, I'm still staring into his eyes.

Did I mention they were blue?

Blue the way mountains are blue in the distance on a hot summer day. Like the sky right after the sun goes down. Blue like the kind of blue that I'm still trying to figure out exactly what shade they are, and that must be why I can't look away from him.

I don't even remember what I was saying.

Although, the bookbag I'm holding is really heavy. What does Melody have in here, rocks?

Even as I ask myself that, I know it's quite possible. She's a science nerd just like I am, only I love biology, not necessarily organic biology but human biology, which is my jam.

If I thought I could actually get a job and raise my kids in Good Grief, I would have been a biology major in college.

But biology majors typically would go on to get postgraduate degrees, and that wasn't something that was happening for me.

I didn't mind at all. I didn't really want any kind of postgraduate degree; I wanted to live in Good Grief far more. I just love biology.

My daughter is much more about inorganic science, hence the rocks.

Regardless, those things get heavy.

Still, I can't figure out where I was in the conversation, and Tammy isn't helping. Trey isn't either, since either he's watching to see what stupid thing I do next, or he's having the same problem with his eyes that I am.

It's probably the first.

You'd think, at this point, things couldn't get any worse.

I'm relatively young, but one thing I have learned in my four decades on this earth. Things can *always* get worse.

I haven't had time yet to introduce you to my dog, Midget.

I say mine, but Midget was one of those things that, when I was still married, my husband took our two girls one afternoon while I was working, and while normally I was always pretty happy when he decided to take some time with them, this time it was a little more difficult for me to be happy, since I got home and was cooking supper when he walked in with two excited little girls and what I thought was a full-grown dog but turned out to be a Great Dane puppy.

The puppy was a surprise to me. The girls I'd been expecting, obviously.

Apparently, Expensive Boobs loved Great Danes—she loved looking at them, since when he left me, he left the dog too—and he was trying to impress her with what a wonderful family man he was by getting the girls a puppy.

If I sound bitter about that, I'm really not. I love Midget. I just don't love the fact that I have her because Cody was trying to impress another woman.

Something I think any normal human would be annoyed about, but I could be wrong.

Anyway, Midget is now the size of a small pony, and she weighs more than I do.

She's also rather standoffish toward men. I kinda think she holds it against my ex that he left her too. Anyway, she loves me. And my girls. And Tammy, which is quite a feat.

I'm kidding about that. I love my sister too. Just sometimes, she's annoying. Like now.

Anyway, Midget is like a typical Great Dane, and she's mostly a couch ornament, except she must have decided after listening to us out on the porch that it was finally time for her to get up and see if there were any intruders she could love to death.

Now, I don't know how much experience you have with Great Danes, but when they get excited, they're kind of like a locomotive. Hard to stop.

Tammy spends so much time at my house she practically lives here. She's been alone for three years since her ex left her, and I think it's easier for her to face her life at my loud and crazy house.

Anyway, as much time as she's here, she should be used to Midget, but maybe she was just too busy watching Trey and I stare at each other.

Whatever it is, she just isn't prepared when Midget comes barreling to the door. Tammy hardly offers any resistance at all since the door pops open, and Midget rumbles out, straight toward me.

I'm not sure if I mentioned this or not, but I'm not very athletic.

I guess this is as good a time as any to mention I'm also the girls' basketball coach at the Good Grief High School as well. It's a long story, and I'll tell that some other time.

Anyway, I know I am going to end up going backward down the three steps because I don't have any hands to ward Midget off.

Most of the time, she doesn't jump up, but when she gets really excited, sometimes she forgets her manners.

She and I are the same that way. I can't hold it against her.

Just like that time at Christmas when I called Cody's new fling Expensive Boobs in front of the kids.

Anyway, maybe coaching basketball has been a little bit good for me, because I do manage to get out of Midget's way before she barrels into me. Unfortunately, as I do, I swing my body around, and Melody's backpack, which I think I might have mentioned is extremely heavy, swings with me.

Now, maybe in a perfect world, that would somehow have thrown me off balance and I would have landed in Trey's arms, and we would realize we are perfect for each other, and all of our problems would vanish, and he would kiss me there in front of my sister and God and everybody, and I'd be planning a wedding right now instead of cringing.

Because that's not what happened at all.

That kind of stuff is for romance novels. Not for real life.

Let me tell you what happens in real life.

Melody's bookbag comes up and slams into my sister, who screams and throws her arms up, losing her balance, taking two large steps forward and crashes into Trey.

Unfortunately, an object in motion tends to stay in motion unless acted upon by an outside force.

Trey is quite a force to crash into, but maybe since he isn't expecting it, he doesn't really stop her forward momentum. In fact, she pushes him backward, right over the railing, and they both flip heels over head and land on their heads and shoulders in the flower bed.

So, most of the time, I try to believe that it's a good idea to be thankful for little things, even in the midst of large catastrophes.

When you get to know my sister a little better, you'll realize that this definitely qualifies as a large catastrophe.

So, I take a nanosecond, and not a hair longer, and am thankful that at least the door is shut, and our cats can't escape.

We have three. One for each daughter and one for my husband. He left it, too, when he walked out.

Anyway, I look over the railing, all traces of any kind of superiority wiped off my face. There's nothing that makes anyone more upset than to be laughed at when something terrible happens to them.

I have a lot of faults. A lot. But one of my faults is not that I laugh at people when bad things happen.

Even though I've never seen my proper, serious sister in quite that position before. Her feet are only about two feet from my nose, and her shoulder is in the dirt, with her head in the mulch beside it right next to Trey's rear end.

I have no idea how they ended up like that, but if I ever laugh at anyone in a catastrophe, that would be it.

I button my lips down tight, and when I'm sure I'm not even going to have a lip twitch, let alone a smile, I say, "Are you guys okay?" I admit I say it kind of short and fast, because while Midget is a great dog, she's never learned to come.

She loves to be outside. But we can't ever let her out without being on a leash, other than in our fenced-in backyard, because she runs away.

So, as much as there are definitely times in my life where I wish I didn't have a giant dog named Midget running around my house, my girls would be devastated if anything happened to her.

Truth be told, I am fond of her too and would probably be more broken up than the girls.

"We're fine. Go get your dog," Tammy says, knowing exactly how Midget is, having had to chase her a time or two herself.

Tammy might be a stickler for details, and she definitely doesn't wear her emotions on her sleeve or her face or anywhere else, but I know she loves that dog. Almost every bit as much as I do.

Trey, having no idea what the big rush is, is slower to respond. But I hear him grunt, and then he says, "I'm upside down in the mulch in your flower bed, and you're asking me if I'm okay?"

"That means he's fine," Tammy says, having had a little experience with men, being that she was married for years and did have two boys.

Now that I'm certain they're both all right, my mind is already racing after my dog. I should check Mrs. Thompson's house first, since when we go for walks, she often feeds Midget scraps. She actually keeps treats in her house for our dog, since she doesn't have a dog of her own, and when Midget gets the opportunity to roam, she typically goes there first.

Since Midget is the only Great Dane in Good Grief, she is a favorite of the residents, because she does stand out. We even hitch her to an old pony cart and let her walk in the parades—there are seven or eight of them every year—and people love it. Anyway, she is super popular, and she has a lot of stops to make, and she knows she has to make them fast before I catch up to her.

I also have a thought in the back of my head that my daughter is cooking and I need to make sure that my house doesn't burn down. I am hoping to catch Midget sooner than later, and without saying anything more to either one of the two adults who are now adjusting their bodies in the flower bed trying to avoid the rose thorns, I set out.

three

. . .

Trey

I'M GOING to admit first thing I've never done anything like that before.

No one who knows me would call me clumsy.

Not even close.

Claire has always done that to me.

Growing up, she'd always been older, and probably like for most teenage boys, she was that beautiful, untouchable, drop-dead gorgeous older woman who was completely off limits to me. Which of course meant that I was absolutely head over heels in love with her from the time I was about six.

I never saw her in school. From what I heard from other people, she was studious and bookish, but I never saw her there.

She was that much older. Not even kidding.

I'd see her in the backyard dancing to her boombox.

Once in a while, I saw her in their hall window, walking past and flinging her hair around, or a couple of times, she had her arms set like she was waltzing with someone invisible.

She just seemed so mysterious and yet at the same time so approachable. She always had a sweet smile and a word or two for me.

I know she was just being nice, but those kind words and smiles fueled all my teenage daydreams.

So, since she was so much older than I was and completely out of my league, when I got to high school, I did the next best thing. I dated her sister.

Her sister wasn't anything like her, and that relationship didn't last long. It lasted longer than maybe it would have if I hadn't put so much effort into keeping it, because I saw Claire more while I was dating Kori than I did at any other time in my life.

I even ate supper with her family a few times. Saw her at holidays.

She graduated from college the same year I graduated from high school, and then I left and never came back. Not for more than a couple weekend visits in the summer maybe.

Eventually, her parents moved out, and she and her husband bought her childhood home and started a family.

I guess when she got married, it should have killed my daydreams. It did mostly. I don't believe in coveting another man's wife, except in my head, she wasn't another man's wife.

Still, once she was married, that meant she'd never be mine, and so by the time I graduated from college, I had a girl, one who is as different from Claire as she could be, and I married her.

Everybody makes mistakes. That was a big one for me.

Now she's got my boys in Florida. Long story.

I'm here in Idaho because my dad had a stroke. He's pretty young for a stroke, mid-50s, but exercise and nutrition are things I've always been interested in, and I thought I could probably help him.

Okay. I'd also heard that Claire lived beside him again. That's a long story too.

Regardless, I don't forget my manners as I manage to get myself up out of the dirt, and instead of chasing after Claire like I want to, I turn around and hold my hand out for Tammy.

Tammy is also older than I am, but she was never interesting to me like Claire.

She grasps it, her fingers long and slender, her eyes—which I admit are a pretty shade of green—don't captivate me the way Claire's do, but I meet them anyway.

"Thank you," she says with more dignity than most women who'd just been lying facedown in the dirt would. One of her feet is still leaning up against the porch wall. She grabs my hand, rights her feet, and stands up.

I was a pretty good ballplayer in high school, like a lot of kids. Partly because I was six feet tall at a young age. Tammy isn't that much shorter than I am, and I don't have to bend my neck to look down at her.

As I recall, Claire is about the same height.

My ex is short.

I guess right there you know that I'm not the smartest dude in the world and certainly not the first one who married a woman who was all wrong for him.

I would have made it work, if only for the kids' sake, but she didn't want to. Or I guess she just found a guy she could love more than me. Or love instead of me.

Whatever. I'm over it.

"You okay?" I ask, dropping my hand. There is no reason to keep a hold of hers. I have a feeling, if it were Claire's hand in mine, I would have tried to find an excuse to hold on.

"I am." Her brows raise as her eyes skim over my face. Has my nose grown? Or can she tell that the high school crush she'd been talking about was actually me? I don't say that, of course. I just wait.

"You look like the rosebushes might have kicked your butt. Or at least your cheek." One of her fingers comes up, and a nail that, because of my years with my ex, I recognize as perfectly manicured tapped her cheek.

As soon as she does it, it is like my brain gets the signal, and my cheek starts burning. I realize something warm and wet is sliding down it.

"I guess that's not going to help my manly reputation any," I joke as one of my hands goes up and I wipe the blood away. "Maybe we can just say I got into a brawl with a biker. Back me up?"

Her eyes crinkle, and she smiles a smile that shows her teeth. "I'd back you, sure, but Claire is a real stickler for the truth, and if she gets wind of it, she'll correct any misconceptions."

I let my eyes crinkle, but I don't really believe what she's saying. As I recall, Tammy is the one who has to have every i dotted and every t crossed.

Regardless, I can admire a woman who won't lie. Actually, it's the only kind of woman I would want. I guess I could add *after what I've been through,* but that just shows how stupid I was to begin with. I should have looked for that from the first and not had to go through the lies in order to want to find one who doesn't.

That saying "older and wiser" certainly applies to me.

"I guess I'd better go help Claire find her dog."

All of the Harding girls are slender as I recall, and Tammy still looks youthful with a willowy figure.

From what I saw of Claire, she seems a little more substantial than she was.

That is good. At least in my mind. Since I am certainly a little more substantial than I was in high school.

I certainly don't have six-pack abs, but I never quite attained those in high school, either.

I would make a better Santa Claus than I would a romance book cover model.

I did a lot of eating after my divorce. Seattle has a lot of great restaurants.

Tammy raises a slender shoulder. I can't help but think that she could use a little meat on her bones. "You don't need to help her. That dumb dog gets out and is predictable as sunrise. Although, she's never knocked anyone off the porch that I know of." She gives a little smile and brushes at the dirt that is still clinging to the seat of her pants as she and I walk around the stairs and stop at the railing.

"So she goes somewhere in particular when she gets out?" I ask.

"First, Mrs. Thompson's house. Mrs. Thompson always gives her treats. Then she has a string of people she visits after that. She has to be fast though, and she knows it, because someone's always on her tail trying to catch up to her. Even in Good Grief, it's not considered a good thing to have your dog running around loose all over town."

"Or your pony apparently." The dog is huge. I recognized it as a Great Dane, and I suppose there were some of those in Seattle, but I didn't typically hang out with dog people. My ex is allergic, and we had cats. She got those, too, in the divorce. And I didn't fight her for them any more than I fought her for the boys. Just something in me said that it wasn't good for kids to see their parents fight, so as much as I didn't think she deserved everything she got, I kept it civil.

Maybe it was a mistake, but I didn't have any examples to follow. My parents stayed married until my mom died in the boating accident.

"The girls used to ride her like she was a pony. But really, Claire can get her."

"Well, if you're okay, I'll just mosey on and make sure. I wanted to talk to her anyway."

Tammy nods, probably remembering that I was at the door specifically asking to talk to Claire.

I manage to keep the smile off my face. She was behind the car, hiding for some reason. Knowing what I do about Claire, that she is slightly goofy and always doing the weirdest things, it is hard to tell what in the world she was doing back there.

The thought that maybe she hadn't wanted to talk to me did go through my head, but it isn't a thought I entertained.

I don't think she would have anything personal against me. It was just one of those crazy things she does, like dancing in her bedroom, flinging her hair around, and doing crazy bubble experiments in the backyard.

She always had some kind of science thing going. One summer, she had three birds with broken wings in cages in her yard.

I assume her parents wouldn't let them in the house, even though her dad is a vet.

I also assume the game commission wasn't interested in whether or not a sparrow with a broken wing lived or died.

Yeah. Claire is definitely different.

"It's good to see you. Don't be a stranger," Tammy says.

As I turned to walk away, I lift my hand in acknowledgment of her words and follow the path that Claire took when she hurried away.

I stride quickly, hoping to catch up.

And before you get the idea that I'm chasing Claire around because I just can't live without her, it's not true.

I admit, and I stand by it, that I did have a huge crush on her in high school.

I also admit, and I stand by this too, that I got a little lost in her eyes.

She really does have amazing eyes.

I can also admit that there's a certain kind of zinging attraction that I feel when I see her.

I just found that out though, since this was the first time I've seen her in forever. So, I haven't quite figured out what to do about that.

But that really isn't the reason I am chasing her down.

I was actually at her house because I need to talk to her about the basketball position.

I'd been told by Mrs. Riley down at the post office that Claire is the basketball coach.

I laughed at this when I first heard it, and Mrs. Riley laughed along. But when I was done laughing and looked at Mrs. Riley, she shrugged and said it was true.

I laughed some more, and she laughed with me, but I realize now she was doing it to be polite.

That's one nice thing about a small town. People are polite.

So anyway, I am following Claire, true. But it's not what you think.

People in a small town are typically honest, and I'm going to be completely honest here. It's a little bit because of what you think. But mostly because I need to talk to her about the basketball position.

Good Grief isn't that big of a town, and Midget takes up half of the town's available real estate when she walks outside, so it can't be that hard to find a pony running around.

I set out in the direction of Mrs. Thompson's house.

She lives on the other side of my dad—and now me, since I am officially moved in.

I don't have a job in town. I kept my job in Seattle, and I'm going to work remotely. There might be a few times I have to drive to the office, but it'll be worth it to be able to be with Dad and take care of him.

I walk through our yard and notice that the grass needs to be mowed. I noticed it a couple of days ago when I first walked up the walk, but there are a lot of things that need to be repaired.

Mowing the grass and doing house repairs isn't exactly my thing.

In my condo in Seattle, I wasn't responsible for any repairs.

Hopefully, my small-town roots will show up sometime. When I was a kid, I mowed plenty of grass.

Mrs. Thompson's house is a pretty yellow one. I remember it as a brighter yellow, but I'm not sure whether the fifteen years I've been away have faded it, or if my memory just dusted it off and sparkled it up.

Regardless, there is no pony galloping through her yard and no green-eyed gorgeous woman chasing after it, so I do what any normal person would do and go around to Mrs. Thompson's back door and knock on it.

I've seen her a couple of times since I moved in, and we talked over the fence, so she knows exactly who I am when she opens the door.

I see Midget in her kitchen, and I smile a little to myself. Claire obviously did not see the dog and went on to the next house.

I have visions of gloating as I take the dog back to her house and wait until she gets there, my prideful look and her gratitude figuring prominently in the images in my head.

"Come on in, neighbor. I was just making cookies when I got a visitor. You make two."

I think at first she is talking about the dog, but as I step into her kitchen, I hear a female voice. "Tammy Harding, you and I need to have a serious talk. I'm pretty sure he had no idea about my crush, and you really embarrassed me. And by the way, the next time I'm hunkered down behind my car, maybe it could occur to you that that's exactly where I want to be? And maybe I was there because I didn't want to talk to him? Hello? Did you think that I wanted to see our neighbor for the first time in fifteen years, the neighbor I had a huge crush on, the all-state basketball star, Good Grief's own claim to fame, with my hair looking like I dropped six bottles of really ugly glue in it and set it on fire?"

I realize as I see Claire's head bent underneath the faucet and the water running over it that maybe there is something a little bit weird going on with her hair, but honestly, if you ever see Claire, you'll know exactly what I mean about those green eyes. They just suck you in, and I couldn't have told you that there was anything weird about her hair.

I know sometimes guys are accused of being a little slow in the thought processing department, and come on, when it comes to girls and their fashions, I am woefully behind the times.

I am still staring at the sink, trying to process what she was saying, when her head lifts up with her hair dripping. Her hands wring the hair out and twist it to the side, and her face tilts. I'm pretty sure she thought she was going to see her sister.

Instead, she sees me.

four

· · ·

Trey

HER EYES GET WIDE, but not as wide as her mouth before it snaps shut along with her eyes and her head goes back in the sink. I think her forehead is resting on the bottom, and I believe she is groaning.

It sounds like she might have had some bad lettuce in her salad for lunch or something.

"Sweetie, your sister isn't here. It's just Trey."

I think Mrs. Thompson is trying to be helpful, and I appreciate that, but I'm pretty sure Claire doesn't. Not if the groaning, which gets louder and more painful sounding, is any indication.

Midget is pretty concerned about her mistress, sniffing around and whining. She bats me with her tail as she goes by, and it feels a little bit like a baseball bat in the kneecap. I think it is an accident, although it does hurt.

She ignores me and shoves her big black nose in Claire's armpit.

And yeah, Claire is pretty tall, but she is bent over the sink and Midget easily reaches her armpit.

The groaning doesn't stop, but it might have gotten a little bit quieter as Claire's arm comes out and goes around the splash of white fur on Midget's neck.

Most of the Great Danes I've seen are brown. But Midget is black with a big white collar and bib and four white paws. She is actually really pretty. Although, her tail really packs a punch.

I thought Claire's groaning was embarrassment, but since it hasn't stopped, I shift my eyes over to look at Mrs. Thompson to see if she is concerned.

She doesn't seem to be, since she is arranging cookies on a plate and acting like there aren't any sounds at all coming from the sink.

"So is there something wrong with your hair that you need some help with?" I ask, and my voice sounds tentative even though I don't mean for it to. I want to be confident and strong, especially since I do kind of, on some level, like Claire.

There's that attraction that I mentioned that I haven't processed yet. It isn't that I want to keep my options open, but it's more I'm thinking I want her to like me. I don't know why. I am not sure I ever want to do that again. My ex came up with so many reasons why I didn't suit her after we were married. It isn't that I don't trust women, exactly, it's just…just I'm not sure whether I want to do that again or not.

The groaning stops. So I must have said the right thing.

But then a sigh echoes in the sink, and if I'm not mistaken, her head is moving up and down. I think she is kind of smacking her forehead off the bottom of it.

Not hard enough to hurt but enough that I think maybe I didn't say the right thing after all.

Good to know that I haven't had a personality change since I moved into Good Grief.

I never said the right thing to my ex either. Not that I am looking at Claire like a potential love interest or anything.

Not exactly.

"Do you want a cookie?" Mrs. Thompson says, smiling at me. For the first time since I walked into her house, I realize that we surprised her to the point where she didn't get a chance to put her teeth in.

Not that I care either way. It is simply I've never seen her without her teeth. That wasn't something I saw too much in the circles I ran in when I was in Seattle, either.

I forgot here in Good Grief, neighbors are almost like family.

That's it. You don't put your teeth in whenever family comes to visit, I guess.

"Thank you," I say, taking a cookie off the plate.

Even when I was growing up, Mrs. Thompson's kids had already moved out of the house. I've eaten plenty of her cookies over the years. They don't have baked goods like this in Seattle.

I know that for a fact and almost take two. But even though neighbors are just like family, my mom wouldn't let me take two cookies.

Mrs. Thompson sets the plate of cookies down on the counter. "Now stop, Claire. You don't look nearly as bad as what you think you do. Wrap that towel around your hair and have yourself a cookie."

Mrs. Thompson talks while she takes the towel that is draped around Claire's shoulders and starts patting down her wet hair.

Claire doesn't move for a moment, almost as though she is thinking about whether or not she is actually going to pull her head out of the sink and stand up, or whether she is just gonna stand there all night.

I try not to smile as she obviously decides to stand up and face the music.

I like that decision.

If I had realized that there was something going on with her hair, would I have followed her?

I know the answer to that question is yes, even if that makes me a bad person. I really do want to get the basketball thing settled.

From what I understand, the team didn't win a single game all year last year nor the year before. If we are going to have any chance at all of whipping Good Grief's girls' basketball team into shape this year, I want to get started on it.

Running drills, shooting drills, endurance runs, sprints, passing techniques, and I absolutely want to spend several practices working solely on footwork.

We need to get started.

I'm not entirely sure I am going to be here next year, but I am entirely sure that the town of Good Grief will expect me to be able to make a champion team out of one that was oh and fifteen last year.

I can do it too, but like I said, I want to get started on it.

So, since I am here and she is here, and from what I understand, she is only teaching the girls' basketball team because she has to, not because she wants to, now is as good a time as any.

Midget steps back when Mrs. Thompson steps in, and now she is back over by me. She can't get her nose in my armpit, but she does stop right in front of me and look up, laying her head on my chest.

I'm not exactly a dog person. I already mentioned my cats, and if I hadn't seen that Midget is pretty much harmless, I think, as big as she was, this would be a little scary.

The look in her eye could be intimidation. But I'm pretty sure it is almost…idol worship.

It makes my chest want to swell up like it might if a room full of people were clapping for me. It also makes me feel warm and almost proud.

That is so weird. But if Midget is doing it to get attention, it works. My hands, without me even thinking about it, both come around and start scratching her behind her ears and stroking down her long head and neck, which is much softer than I expected. Almost silky.

Her eyes close, and I know I've been taken.

Intimidation, admiration, total idol worship… Yeah, the dog isn't above doing what she has to do in order to get what she wants. She is obviously in dog heaven with me scratching her.

Still, that keeps her from smacking my knee again with her tail, and since I haven't recovered from the last time, I guess I'm good for it.

"You look just fine, dear. Plus, Trey's a lot older than he used to be, and I'm pretty sure he's figured out that what a woman looks like on the inside is far more important than what she looks like on the outside."

"I don't think men ever figure that out," Claire mutters. "It doesn't matter how old they are. Especially not sportsmen." Claire's voice doesn't exactly sound bitter, but she does sound pretty sure of herself.

"Trey was always different than those other boys. He didn't chase after the pretty ones."

"He did too. He dated Kori for a year or better."

"Ladies." I clear my throat. Although I do continue to scratch Midget. "Ladies. I'm right here."

Mrs. Thompson looks over at me, and she does actually look surprised. I guess she is kind of old, but I can't believe she just offered me a cookie then completely forgot about my presence in her kitchen.

As for Claire... Those amazing eyes go to mine, and I know she hasn't forgotten for one second that I am there. Not any more than I've forgotten about her.

Have I talked about her green eyes yet?

They're magnetic. Or maybe it's Claire that's magnetic, and her eyes are like hooks. I don't know. Whatever they are, I can't pull my eyes away, and I can't think of anything to say either.

"Oh my goodness, Trey. You're still here, and it looks like you're done with your cookie. Have another one." Mrs. Thompson nods her head at the plate of cookies still on the counter. Both of her hands are still on Claire's head doing something with the towel.

Claire is doing something with the towel too, and I'm not sure they are working together, but I know better than to step into that.

I grab a cookie and figure now is as good a time as any to approach the basketball thing.

I need to think about the attraction, figure out what is causing it and what to do about it, but I can't do that standing here in Mrs. Thompson's kitchen with Claire looking at me.

Even if she does have a towel on her head, it doesn't cover those eyes.

They are gorgeous. Seattle might be the Emerald City, but it doesn't have anything on Claire Harding's eyes.

Except she isn't Claire Harding anymore, and maybe she feels the same way about men that I do about women. Or maybe I don't feel that way about all women. At least not about women with gorgeous green eyes and cute button noses, red lips that aren't exactly cherry red but have that little dip in them right in the middle that kind of makes them look like they have a little heart at the top.

Not that I ever looked at women's lips and thought about hearts before.

Definitely I need to start thinking about basketball. It is pretty dangerous to start thinking about lips and hearts and button noses.

Especially when they're all sitting right below those eyes that I can't stop thinking about.

"Of course he's still here. I've embarrassed myself about six thousand times so far in the last fifteen minutes, and I'm sure he's just hanging around to see what pathetic, ridiculous thing I'm going to do next. Good Grief is pretty tame compared to the big city, and I guess he needs his entertainment for the evening."

"I'm still here. You can nicely talk *to* me and not *about* me," I say, irritated for some reason that her eyes are saying one thing but her mouth is saying something else.

I hate it when women do that. It confuses me.

"Are you going to tell me that there's some other reason you're here? Standing in Mrs. Thompson's kitchen? With my dog, and staring at me like I have horns and a forked tongue?"

She has me hot now, and my mouth moves faster than my brain. Never a good thing. "Actually, there is. I'm going to coach the girls' basketball team this year, and I need you to tell Mrs. Pinkerton, the principal at Good Grief, so she can inform the school board that I'm taking over your job. The sooner, the better."

That isn't exactly how I meant to say that.

She's right, I was staring at her. Not exactly how she said but still in an embarrassing way. And I am embarrassed, and annoyed because she was doing that whole look one way while lips say something else thing, and also irritated because I don't mind petting Midget but she pretty much soaked the entire front of my shirt.

I wasn't expecting that.

Not that I particularly mind, but I don't want to deal with Claire, whom I am feeling rather attracted to, and who obviously doesn't like me even a little, with dog slobber all over the front of my shirt.

And of course, Midget, as soon as she hears Claire's voice, leaves me—and the big wet spot on the front of my shirt—and strides over to her mistress, who she obviously adores.

"I'll do no such thing. The girls' basketball team is mine. I'm not going to go to Mrs. Pinkerton and tell her that you're coaching when I fully intend to," she says.

I had thought I sounded irritated. Claire really sounds irritated.

I continue, thinking, despite my previous experience with women, that my reasonable argument will win her over. "Mrs. Riley said that you didn't even want to coach the team. I'm doing it as a favor for you. You're supposed to be happy."

Okay, I know that isn't exactly the best way to phrase anything either, but for some reason, none of the stuff that is coming out of my mouth is how I would have said it on a normal day.

Apparently, today is not a normal day for me.

Obviously, since I don't typically have dog slobber down the front of my shirt.

Dog slobber isn't exactly in the men's manual on how to win a woman.

"I love coaching basketball. The girls love me. And I've been doing it for three years now. I have no intentions of giving it up. Especially not to you." She says this as she flips the towel around her hair, making some kind of castle thing with it on top of her head, and I might add it doesn't detract at all from the greenness of her eyes.

It might seem like I am a little obsessed with her eyes.

That's true. I am.

So of course, I don't magically revert back to my regular self, but no, I continue to be a crazy man who can't manage to say anything nice to the girl he's attracted to, and more things I normally would never say pour out of my mouth. "You don't know anything about basketball. You always ran around with your nose in a book. Unless you were doing some kind of weird science experiment. Do you even know what a basketball looks like? Have you ever even played basketball?"

"Of course I do." Claire's eyes are narrowed, and while I still admire them, I'm also slightly uncomfortable. "A basketball is two triangles glued together, one pink, one green. If you can find them small enough, you can wear them on a ring on your finger. If you examine them under a microscope, they look very similar to a single-celled organism with a nucleus. That's on a good day. On a bad day, they have small nematodes pointing out of them, very similar to your chin."

I'm not sure exactly what she just said but am pretty sure she insulted me.

In a rather scientific way.

I wasn't a deadbeat in school, but math was my thing. I actually went to school for business.

"So obviously, you don't know what a basketball looks like," I say, allowing myself a little smirk but not really meaning it.

"I was being sarcastic," she says, softer than she was speaking. Almost like maybe she is feeling a little bad for being unkind. I'm not going to give her that luxury though.

"I've been gone for a long time. I hadn't realized small towns had gotten so nasty."

"Oh, Trey. Have a cookie." Mrs. Thompson steps between us. There is barely enough room for her to fit. I have no idea when either one of us stepped closer to the other. We almost look like we're getting ready to have a tipoff at the beginning of a ball game, that's how close we are.

I don't think she was any more aware of that than I was, because she looks just as surprised as I feel.

Mrs. Thompson, looking a little unsure for the first time, glances between the two of us as I pick a cookie from the tray she's holding.

"You too, Claire. Have a cookie."

five

. . .

Trey

I'M sure the sound I hear is Claire's teeth grinding together, but she lifts her lips and shows her teeth—and I suppose in some circles you could term that a smile—as her fingers come up and she picks a cookie from the tray.

"Thank you, Mrs. Thompson. Your cookies are delicious."

I smile at that, because Claire is obviously talking with her teeth ground together. In fact, her lips barely move.

That's kind of how I feel, though. I've been told she doesn't want to coach the basketball team, and I also know, as much as I had a huge crush on her, that she skipped gym class as often as she could and wouldn't know a ball if it hit her in the forehead. Truly.

I'm not saying that in a mean way, because really, she can dissect frogs in circles around me. The idea of cutting a frog open makes me want to throw up.

The idea of cutting any animal open makes me want to throw up. I definitely couldn't be a nurse. So my hat's off to her, for the most part.

It has been my experience with my ex that if I give her credit, she will take it and completely ignore the idea of reciprocation.

Maybe I should reexamine that expectation of mine.

After all, I'm pretty sure when I give someone credit, I'm not supposed to expect any in return.

But isn't it human to want that?

Or maybe it's male.

"Are you seriously gonna tell me that you really do want to coach the girls' basketball team?" I say, and I hope my tone is conciliatory, almost a *let's put this behind us and get along* kind of tone. That's what I'm going for anyway. That's how I feel really. I don't want to fight. Not with Claire. I'm not really a fighter in any case, but Claire would be my last choice.

There are plenty of other things I'd like to do with her.

That thought kind of comes out of nowhere, and I'm not sure exactly what it means.

"I do." She lifts her chin, like she is challenging me, but the effect is honestly kind of ruined because she has a cookie crumb stuck to her lip.

I don't believe her for a second. I can tell, by the little flicker in her eyes, she doesn't believe herself either. I could be wrong, but I think she's wondering why she's even bothering to argue with me.

We both know she doesn't really want to coach.

I haven't seen her for years, but I'm pretty sure she didn't develop a serious interest in basketball since the last time, combined with the rumors I've heard, especially.

Regardless, I grind my teeth together. I had been counting on that coaching position to relieve some of the boredom of being back in my small hometown. To replace evenings at the gym and Saturdays on the golf course.

Seattle wasn't exactly a sport-centric city, but I stayed active and engaged.

I had definitely been excited about the coaching position when I'd spoken with Mrs. Pinkerton.

She was fairly sure that Claire would give it up in a heartbeat.

Apparently, there'd been some arm-twisting going on when Claire was given the position.

I inquired about the boys' team but was shut down immediately. It was full, and there were three assistant coaches.

"Do you even like basketball?" The question is out of my mouth before I could think about it. It is the one that is running through my head. The one I am sure I know the answer to. The one I know was a definite "no" from the Claire I knew in high school.

"It doesn't matter. I'm the coach. I've been the coach for the last three years, and just because the hotshot baller from high school is back in town doesn't mean I'm going to give up my position or walk away from it. Those girls mean something to me."

"They'll mean something to me too." Eventually. I'm sure I will get to know them and care for them.

Her arms cross over her chest, and her foot taps on the floor. The effect is slightly ruined by the towel tower that is stacked on top of her head. And the crumb on her lip.

Have you ever been talking to someone with a crumb on their lip and been tempted to brush it off with your finger?

I never have.

Not until this very moment. It's a really weird temptation. One that kind of makes me stop and take a step back and look at myself up and down like what in the world has gotten into me?

I admit I lose the thread of the conversation.

My eyes are definitely hooked on her lips.

I am looking at the crumb. Honest. Not actually, you know, looking at her lips because they are appealing or attractive or anything.

Well, they are appealing and attractive, but that's not why I am looking at them. Anyway, she kinda surprises me when she says, "I think you have ulterior motives."

It takes a moment for that to sink in, and then I tear my eyes from the crumb on her lip and meet her gaze.

"Like what?"

Surely she doesn't know I am actually thinking about kissing her. Not that I want to, I am just thinking about it.

"I think all you're interested in is winning a championship. There's more to sports than winning. It's about character growth and development and those girls' potential beyond the court. I don't think you see that."

Okay. I guess this is where I admit she is right. I don't see that. I mean of course I think character growth is important. And I think sports teach character. But come on, who doesn't want to win a championship? That isn't an ulterior motive for coach. That *is* the motive.

But her stance says she thinks there is something wrong with wanting to win.

How do I argue with that?

It takes me about three seconds to figure out the answer to that question. I don't.

You can't argue with a person who doesn't use logic.

"If you give me the head coach position, you can have the assistant coach position." That wasn't exactly what the principal had told me. She'd said that if Claire wouldn't give me the head coach position, *I* could have the assistant coach position, which currently is unfilled. But the principal assured me that Claire is handling the coaching duties as well as anyone could expect and she hasn't really needed an assistant coach.

With an oh and fifteen record for last year, I didn't think anybody was doing anything competently in regards to the girls' basketball team, but I hadn't said that during our conversation.

Claire is already shaking her head. "There really isn't any need for an assistant coach. I'm fine coaching by myself. Completely happy. Maybe they'll give you a spot on the boys' team."

"Already asked. It's full." Normally in a conversation like this, I wouldn't have said that. Wouldn't have admitted that rejection which equals weakness. But even though I feel like Claire and I are antagonizing each other, I don't think we are enemies. I also don't feel like Claire is the kind of person who would use that kind of knowledge against me.

Turns out I am right about that.

She nods, like she'd known.

"But Mrs. Pinkerton seems to think you don't really enjoy coaching."

"Mrs. Pinkerton is wrong." Claire's arms are still crossed tight over her chest, and her lips button down tight after she says that.

A familiar throbbing starts to push between my eyes, and I pinch the bridge of my nose.

I honestly came back for my dad's health, but I am having migraines, have been fighting them for a year, and suspect they are stress related. Because, like now, in the middle of what could loosely be termed an argument, they always start.

This isn't a migraine though; it's just a regular run-of-the-mill headache. That could trigger a migraine.

"That's fine. I won't argue with you about it anymore."

"Thank you. I appreciate it." Claire seems pleased.

"I'll take the assistant position." I reach in my pocket and pull out my phone. "Give me your number, and I'll send you a text. You can let me know what time the practices are, and we can get together and talk about our expectations and goals for the year and how we're going to accomplish them."

I think everything I am saying is pretty run-of-the-mill, and I think I am being pretty magnanimous by giving in and letting her win our fight. It is a shock to me when I hold my phone and there is silence from her.

I look up. Her eyes are narrowed. That is the only change in her position.

"Now what?" The words come out wearily, because my head is really starting to hurt.

She breathes in and out, as though wanting to say that she should have some say in who is her assistant coach, but we both know that she really doesn't. The school district isn't going to turn me down. I am, after all, the most successful basketball player to ever set foot in Good Grief High.

"The first game isn't until just before Thanksgiving. We'll start practices that week. I'm sure I'll see you before that, but until then, there's no need for you to have my number."

Okay. I admit. I laugh. I think she is joking. I mean come on, she *is* joking, right?

She doesn't laugh.

Midget, who had parked herself in Mrs. Thompson's spot between us, looks between both of us and whines, as though wanting to emphasize the gravity of the situation.

So she isn't joking?

I pinch the bridge of my nose again, which has done nothing for my headache, and then run a hand over the top of my head. I keep it cut short, because my hairline is slowly working its way back the sides of my skull, and I really hate seeing my forehead grow in the mirror every morning.

Just one more reminder that I am growing old.

Which has nothing to do with this argument, other than maybe when I was younger, I would have dug in and gotten what I wanted.

I'm not quite the fighter now that I was then. But I can't let this go.

"That's fine. If you don't want to bother with practices, I'll do it myself. Just let me know if you want to keep in touch with what I'm doing. I will assume when you give me your phone number, you want updates."

"You can't do that."

"I sure can."

"I'm the coach. I'm in charge of the practices."

"You'll be in charge of the practices when you decide to start coaching. But if you're not having any, you've abdicated your responsibility, and I'll pick up your slack. That's what the assistant coach does. So I'll run the practices until you're ready to start in November." If I do that, we might actually have a chance at winning something this year. I hope she just lets it go.

I should have known better.

"Fine." She rattles off her number.

I'm not expecting it. I had dropped my hand that is holding my phone down to my side. It's gone blank.

By the time I get it turned on and start putting her number in, I've forgotten the last four digits. She has to repeat them, which I'm not too happy about but don't have a choice.

"I need to get home. My daughter is cooking supper, and I've been away long enough." Her hand goes up like she's going to adjust the towel on her head, but it drops back to her side without touching anything. Her expression becomes stern. "You and I need to talk about these practices and what we're going to be doing. I understand you're very busy, so I'll let you know when I've called the first practice."

Her words are said with confidence, but she is looking down at the kitchen counter like she knows I am right and more practicing will probably produce a better team. Because come on, what kid wants to play on a team that doesn't win a single game? She certainly doesn't seem like she is going to acknowledge that, and I can't blame her.

She grabs a hold of Midget's collar and goes to walk around me.

"We can talk about it on the walk home," I say. I don't want her to weasel out of it. Even though I have her number now, if she's not going to talk to me about it, I am seriously going to call my own practices.

Claire opens her mouth, but I never find out what she is going to say.

"Oh, honey, I was hoping you could stay and look at my sink. It's leaking." Mrs. Thompson stands with both hands underneath a paper plate filled with cookies, artfully arranged, with what looks like a slab of Jell-O in the middle. They are covered with plastic wrap. Little toothpicks hold the plastic up from the shiny stuff in the middle.

Thankfully, she is holding it out to Claire. But as I look away, I realize that's what Mrs. Thompson was doing at the counter while Claire and I were having our discussion. There is a plate for—I assume—me, too.

I shift, aware of my loafers and the business suit I'm wearing. I took my tie off and unbuttoned the top button, but still, I am sure normal people wouldn't pass me off as a plumber.

But normal people are few and far between in Good Grief, Idaho.

Normal people live in New York or California. Somewhere warm. Somewhere with lots of nice restaurants and no green-eyed girls that make my heart pound.

"I'll take a look at it, Mrs. Thompson. Although I'm not making any promises." I did a lot of work for my dad growing up, but plumbing isn't exactly my area of expertise.

I didn't take a single plumbing class in college. Although I took plenty of classes that seemed completely worthless. Russian history comes to mind.

A plumbing class would have been much more beneficial.

I don't think the money I spent in college was meant to actually pay for anything useful.

Claire, with one hand still gripping Midget's collar, slides her hand under the plate that Mrs. Thompson holds.

I think she was going to leave.

"Claire. If you can wait a few minutes, I'll walk home with you and we can have that discussion."

"I told you, I need to leave. My daughter's cooking, and I need to go make sure she doesn't catch the kitchen on fire."

I think she is serious.

"Your mom's the fire chief. I'm sure she has everything under control."

"*Because* my mom is the fire chief, I need to make sure my daughter doesn't catch the kitchen on fire." This is the first time that I notice something that might be humor on her face.

I don't remember her smiling too much when we were younger. I didn't see her in school, but she struck me as a serious student. At home, she was a little more unbridled, and I think there is a goofy personality lurking underneath all of that super serious stuffy stuff she projects to the world.

The idea that that might be true jacks up the attraction I've been feeling all along. It isn't an unpleasant feeling, but it certainly is unwelcome.

She's kind of right. I have colleagues that I will still be working with, remotely of course, back in Seattle. They laughed when I said I was moving back to my hometown.

For goodness sakes, I never called my hometown Good Grief. Not to my business colleagues. They thought I was moving to the sticks, and they were pretty much right. They thought I was going backward in my career, and they were kind of right about that too.

In doing what I've done, there isn't too much of my life that can be respected or admired from a business/personal point of view.

However, success with the girls' basketball team, even modest success, but especially if we win a championship, would more than make up for it.

So yeah, I do kind of have ulterior motives.

No pressure.

It is just my reputation at stake.

Maybe there is a bit of a desperate look on my face, because Mrs. Thompson has compassion on me. "Maybe you could just come back later tonight or tomorrow and take a look at it for me."

I nod. Me taking a look at it will probably consist of me lying down on the floor underneath her sink, getting dirty and putting my back out of joint, and all just so that I can say, "Mrs. Thompson, your sink is leaking." Because I certainly won't have any better idea of how to fix it when I lie down and look at it than I do right now.

"I'll do that," I say. I take the paper plate with my cookies and Jell-O square and wave a thank you with my elbow as I hurry out the door after Claire.

six

. . .

Claire

SERIOUSLY? Is the dude following me?

I've already made it down the porch steps and to Mrs. Thompson's gate before I hear what sounds like footsteps on her back stairs. The ones I just went down.

He is. He's following me.

I thought he was going to look at her sink. I figured I could make a clean getaway.

Midget doesn't walk very well on a leash, and it's almost impossible to grab a hold of her collar and lead her anywhere. She is basically dragging me while I try hard to keep the plate of cookies level.

I guess I like Jell-O, but I don't typically like it mixed up with cookies, and I definitely don't like soggy cookies.

I'm pretty sure it's Jell-O in the middle of the cookies. Hence, my desperation to keep the plate level.

Still, I can't resist tilting my head over my shoulder as we go through the gate and hook a hard left back to my house.

I should never have done that. I do find out that Trey is indeed following me, but I also hook my foot on the corner post of the fence.

I think I'd have been okay if I hadn't had a hold of Midget's collar.

Or I might have been okay if the fence weren't as old as Mrs. Thompson.

All right. I know I'm not fooling anyone.

I would have been okay if I weren't a clumsy klutz who can't walk in a straight line even without a Great Dane dragging me and a plate of cookies to try to keep level and this overpowering urge to look at Trey Haywood.

As I fall, I let go of Midget's collar, thinking I might be able to catch myself with a hand on the ground, but that doesn't work out because the fence falls down beside me and I end up scraping my shoulder on the pointy tops while trying to get away from it and also keep the cookies level. In hindsight, I should have just given up on the cookies. I end up twisting and somehow landing on my back on top of the fence, with the cookies on the ground.

The good thing about all this is Midget doesn't run away, because she is too busy eating the cookies. Apparently, she likes Jell-O too. And also apparently, she doesn't care whether it's mixed up with her cookies.

So, right. I feel like an idiot.

It's even worse since I just had a huge argument about whether or not I should be the basketball coach, and here I am not even able to put one foot in front of the other without landing on top of someone's fence.

I'm a big believer in if you fall down, you get right back up and try again.

I have to admit I'm also a big believer in lying there for a minute, allowing yourself a chance to catch your breath. Which is what I am doing. With my eyes closed.

I suppose somewhere deep down inside, I am hoping that Trey will just walk on by.

"I suppose Mrs. Thompson is going to want me to take a look at this right after I take a look at the leaky sink."

I don't really want to open my eyes. How is his voice able to send shivers from the base of my skull clear down to the tip of my tailbone and have them trickle right back up feeling just as good the second time?

I don't even like him.

I've learned in the last half hour that it is quite possible to not like someone but have their voice absolutely give you the most amazing case of goosebumps ever recorded in the modern world.

Funny that case is in Good Grief, Idaho. Our sole claim to fame, and only I know about it.

I'm in no hurry to answer him, although what he said doesn't really require an answer, so I leave my eyes closed and wait for the very last of the goosebumps to dissipate before I break the spell and open them.

He's staring straight down at me, holding his own plate carefully in his hand. I'm betting he has the same issues with Jell-O and cookies that I do.

Just guessing.

Thinking of that, I reach out and, because of the mouth noises—Midget is a noisy eater—I know exactly where she is and hook my fingers on her collar.

That's going to make it even more awkward to stand up, but at least I won't be chasing my dog around the neighborhood again. Actually, after she finishes up the plate of cookies, she'll probably be ready to go home anyway.

"I hope Mrs. Thompson isn't watching out of her window. I feel bad that she went through all the trouble to bake the cookies and give me a plate, only to have Midget end up eating them."

I've barely said that when I hear a door slam, the sound of a screen door slapping against the frame, and footsteps on Mrs. Thompson's back stairs.

Trey puts a hand in his pocket and shifts slightly, as though settling himself to stay a while. "Pretty sure she saw it. Pretty sure she's fixing it. Pretty sure you're going to get two plates for your trouble."

I go back to ignoring the shivers the man's voice is giving me.

I roll to my side, still holding on to Midget, hoping I can get up with the least amount of awkwardness possible.

It takes two tries with my limited mobility and also because Midget suddenly notices the one cookie that landed away from the other ones and jerks to get that one just as I'm crawling to my knees.

I don't quite land on my stomach again, but I definitely don't look like a competent basketball coach either.

Not that I ever did.

Still, I'm not going to give up my position to some big shot baller from high school who waltzed in and has everyone else in the town wrapped around his little finger just because he was an all-state champion twenty years ago.

Who will probably be gone next year this time, and I'll have to pick up his pieces.

Right. I'm sure he won't leave the ball team in pieces. And yeah, most of my bad attitude is probably because I know he'll be able to do basketball better than I ever could dream about doing basketball.

But in my defense, I do a lot of things with the team that are not just about basketball. I couldn't explain that to him, because while I'm sure the man is great at basketball, I don't think he appreciates everything that I think is important in life.

It is just easier not even to get into that argument.

And yes, one of the things I try to teach the team is that easier is not always better.

Sometimes, I don't always practice what I preach.

Like now.

I stumble up, tripping over the downed fence, but thankfully, Midget keeps me from falling yet again as I slam into her.

She grunts, and yes, Great Danes grunt, and takes two or three steps to the side before she recovers and steadies herself. Thankfully, she's old enough that she doesn't think I'm trying to play a game with her.

I steady myself on her, and she goes back to the cookies while Mrs. Thompson comes to the fence.

"I'm so sorry about your fence, Mrs. Thompson," I say.

"I know you didn't mean to run into it," Mrs. Thompson says, holding both plates of cookies in my direction. Unfortunately, I only have one hand.

I slide my hand under one of the plates. "Thank you so much. Sorry about the cookies too."

"Oh, don't worry about it. These things happen."

Mrs. Thompson's eyes slant toward Trey, and because I'm normally nice but I do have a shallow brat living in my head, I say, just a little slyly, "Maybe, if Trey is feeling super-duper nice, when he comes over to look at your leaky sink, he'll take a look at this fence and maybe set it back up and fix it."

Okay, I know that might sound dumb, because I really have no clue what it's going to take to fix that fence. I'm guessing Trey doesn't have any more clue on how to fix the fence than he does on how to fix the sink, but since I wouldn't have run into the fence without him chasing me, I do feel like it's only fair that both of us should be responsible for fixing it.

Like I thought it out loud, he says, "I suppose, since you are the one who knocked it down, I could possibly accompany you when you choose to come over and fix it for Mrs. Thompson."

And then I know exactly what I'm going to do with the fence.

I smile. "Of course. Let's make our first basketball practice here. And the girls will learn teamwork as we fix Mrs. Thompson's fence." His eyes narrow, and it's not hard to read displeasure on his face. "And her sink," I add.

It's my equivalent of offering an olive branch.

He doesn't really take it, just jerks his head.

Mrs. Thompson either doesn't feel the undercurrent or chooses to ignore it. "Since you're heading in that direction, do you mind carrying Claire's extra plate of cookies?" she asks, holding the plate out. Her timing isn't the best, but Trey still takes it with his empty hand.

I'm okay with that. I can tell from the way he is holding his own plate that he'll be careful not to let the cookies slide around and touch the Jell-O.

He might be a bit of a stick-in-the-mud, but even stick-in-the-muds have their places. And carrying two plates of cookies with Jell-O in the middle is a very good job for someone who is slightly OCD, which I'm suspecting that Trey is.

I almost smile.

"I guess we'll try this again, Mrs. Thompson. Thank you so much for the cookies and have a nice evening," I say. Midget has finished up the last of the cookies and is once again pulling on my hand, now all of a sudden in a big rush to get home.

I kind of am too. I mentioned about the house burning down. Even though we're only five houses down from the fire station and four houses down from my mom, who sold our family home to Cody and me when we married and bought the house directly beside the fire station.

If there's one thing my mom takes seriously in life, it's being fire chief.

Which is not exactly the reason I don't want her at my house, but it's still a good one.

seven

. . .

Claire

WE WALK ABOUT five steps before Trey says, "Are you sure you're okay? That was quite a fall."

I don't want him to be nice. I want him to be a jerk. I want him to be not what he looks like, which is a handsome middle-aged man who carries himself with confidence and has gorgeous blue eyes, a voice that gives me goosebumps every time he opens his mouth, and a smile that makes me forget my name.

If he's a jerk, I can forget all of those other things, but if he's nice, it's only going to add to my problem.

If he's going to be my assistant coach, it's going to make everything awkward.

Is it terrible to wish he was a jerk?

"So, I'm getting worried. You didn't answer me. Is there something seriously wrong? You're not walking on a broken leg, are you?"

I grunt a laugh over that and resist the urge to slant my eyes to his.

No.

He cannot be funny.

If he's nice *and* funny, I'm done. *So* done.

High school crush all over again.

At least our age difference isn't as terrible now as it was back then. Normal high school seniors don't crush on a kid in junior high.

That's just weird.

"No, I'm fine. Mostly. My pride's a little ragged right now, but I suppose it serves me right." If he's going to be nice, and even if he's not, I need to be. Normally, nice is just a part of my nature. "I'm sorry I was such a jerk about the basketball position." I try not to mumble. "I'm not a great basketball player." I lift a shoulder because my hands are full. Thankfully, Midget isn't pulling me as hard as she was. I think I'd be safe with letting her go, but I don't want to take that chance. "But I really do enjoy working with the girls. And yeah, I haven't been that successful in winning games, but I feel like there's more to sports than just winning."

He blows a short breath out between his lips, as though my comment about more than winning is a little bit ridiculous.

To his credit though, he doesn't argue with me.

I wish he would. I could handle that better than *nice*.

"I think there's always character lessons to be learned in sports. Hard work. Sacrifice. Determination. Willingness to give your all and fight until the buzzer. So I think we're in agreement on that." Trey speaks with the true belief of one who is totally invested in everything he is saying.

While I agree about the character traits he admires, I'm not necessarily in agreement with how one gets those traits.

I never emphasize fighting to the buzzer and all that other rot.

I am all about good sportsmanship and being kind to the other team.

You know, we don't fight, we don't yank the ball away from people, if someone trips, we stop and help them up, even if it means we lose the ball or that the other team scores. Life is all about others and being kind. That's my focus with the basketball team.

Our practices probably look slightly different than what he's thinking too.

If the girls actually help with Mrs. Thompson's fence, it will not be the first time we've had a practice outside of the gym.

We've had a lot of practices in nursing homes.

We leave the basketball at home, and more often than not, we play wheelchair square dancing or cutthroat games of bingo.

I'm thinking Trey won't be impressed.

Maybe I should have a little chat with the girls before he shows up at practice.

I'm still pretty sure Trey isn't serious about this basketball thing and that he won't be staying in Good Grief long.

I know one way to find out.

"So," I say, trying to sound casual. "How long do you think you'll be staying in Good Grief?"

Yeah, that sounded totally innocent and just like I'm talking about the weather. I congratulate myself on my ability to be devious without seeming like it.

"You're wondering how long you have to put up with me as assistant coach?"

Right. Trey saw right through that. I never was a good actress.

I suppose the next thing the school will ask me to be is the drama coach.

Lovely. I'll do that just as well as I do basketball.

Less pressure though. Drama isn't as much about the money as sports are.

eight

. . .

Trey

I HAVE a plate of cookies in each hand, and I'm walking along beside Claire, a little bemused. I'm not sure I've ever been with a person who seems to be able to get herself into predicaments the way Claire has this evening.

Is this the way it always is with her?

Even though there is still some irritation tripping along inside of me over the basketball position, I really understand.

I didn't approach this the best way.

If I was doing something, even if it wasn't something I like to do, I wouldn't want someone coming in and pushing me out of the way. I hadn't been thinking.

I guess my focus was on what I wanted and on assuming she didn't want to do it anyway.

I could have phrased it all a lot nicer.

We don't talk as we walk along, but it's not an awkward silence. It feels kind of peaceful. Especially after how we kind of argued and with all the scrapes we've been in.

I've been in the business world long enough to know that silence is not considered golden. People who have the most animated conversations are the winners.

I don't know why. Seems like it's better to not talk than to just say a bunch of stuff that doesn't need to be said.

Two cars pass us, their headlights on as dusk has fallen, and Claire waves at them both.

Whether or not she knows them, I don't know, but I remember that this is the way it is in small towns. Everyone waves at everyone regardless of whether or not they know them.

I'm assuming neither one of the two people she waved at recognized her with that towel on her head. But I don't know. Maybe that's the way she normally walks around town.

"Was that why you were hiding?" I say, not really planning to.

"What?" She scrunches her brows up and looks at me. It's hard for me not to smile at the towel on her head. The one she seems to have forgotten about.

"Whatever was going on with your hair."

She looks away, back to the front as though watching where her feet are going and focusing on balancing her plate of cookies.

Midget seems to have calmed down. Maybe it's nap time. Not that I have any idea. I've never had a dog, not even growing up.

If I were to get one, it would be one about the size of Midget's front leg.

I almost think Claire isn't going to answer me. But then she says, "I know. Stupid. But yeah. I have my dad's white hair and have since... well, I pulled the first gray strands out in high school. But I didn't start dyeing it until I was almost thirty. Guess I was just being vain and didn't want anyone to see me with the dye in my hair. In hindsight, not my brightest moment."

"No. I get it. I guess we all have things we kinda try to hide as we age." I like that she's told me the truth. I feel like I can reciprocate. Or maybe I just feel safe with her. "My abs are kinda going to flab, and I definitely would have been hiding behind my car if I had been walking around outside without a shirt on."

She grunts a laugh, almost as though she doesn't really believe me. And yeah, she's probably right. I'm definitely a little more sensitive about my midsection than I used to be, but I don't think I would hide because of it. I do know from experience that men are a lot less sensitive about those kinds of things than ladies are.

"I guess it's nice to know that you're human after all."

"Me? Human? Was there ever any doubt?"

"You were the gorgeous older neighbor. Of course, there was doubt." I close my mouth, unwilling to say more.

I never find out what she might have said at that, because as I look up, it's not so dark that I can't see that there's actually smoke coming from the direction of her house. "I thought you were joking about your house catching on fire," I murmur.

She gasps, and her whole body jerks.

I'm pretty sure her Jell-O is now touching her cookies. I'm pretty sure she also doesn't care. "I wasn't joking. Melody is so much like me. She needs someone standing over top of her to remind her to pay attention to stuff, or else she forgets what she was doing."

Her words are rushed, and she starts half walking, half jogging toward her house. It's an awkward kind of movement with the dog and the cookies.

If she were truly worried about her house burning down, I would think she would have dropped the cookies and let go of the dog, but maybe she's just not thinking.

As we get closer, it looks like most of the smoke is pouring out the side door, the one that connects directly to the kitchen.

Yeah. It's open, and her sister from earlier, Tammy, is standing in the doorway waving a dish towel.

"She wouldn't be standing there pushing the smoke out if there was still fire to deal with," I say, mostly to calm Claire down, because I feel like I should be helping her with something, but with a plate of cookies in each hand, I'm pretty useless.

"You're right." She lets out a deep breath. "My heart is still in my throat though. Man, that takes years off your life to think your house is on fire and your kid might be in there."

"If it's any consolation, I was ready to drop the cookies and go in with you. That's saying something, because Mrs. Thompson's cookies are delicious."

She shoots me a look, the corners of her mouth turned up like I want them to be. Man, she sure is a walking catastrophe.

"Is this the way your life usually goes?" I ask, not really making conversation. Truly curious.

"It's a lot of excitement for a small town, isn't it?" she asks, neatly avoiding the question and with more than a little irony in her voice.

"It's a lot of excitement for one person, in any town," I say, meaning it.

"Claire!" Tammy cries, like she hasn't seen her sister in years. "I honestly was keeping an eye on Melody. But I have these papers to correct, and you would not believe some of the answers I'm getting. Kids, in ninth grade, who don't know what a gerund is. Have you ever heard of such a thing?"

It doesn't surprise me that Tammy is an English teacher. She sounds serious too. Which I feel anyone who has been teaching more than five minutes should know there are *always* kids who don't know what a gerund is.

I suck in my stomach, trying to become smaller and fit into Claire's shadow. Hopefully, Tammy isn't going to throw a pop quiz in my direction and ask me what a gerund is.

I have no idea.

All I know is you can't eat it. That makes me uninterested.

I'm guessing that's probably how most of the male population in Idaho and the rest of the United States feels.

I could be wrong.

Although the thought that her house might burn down has been obliterated, the copious amounts of smoke, combined with the fact that there is probably adrenaline pouring through both of us right now, means that we don't really slow down.

We both rush up the stairs of the back porch.

Tammy gives me an odd look. I give her a little smile, still unsure what a gerund is, and say, "Looks like you survived that fall okay."

She grins, a little sheepishly, I think. She's not the kind of person who typically has experiences like that, unless I miss my guess. Maybe it's just my personal bias, but I have a tendency to think of English teachers as dry and mostly boring.

Anyone who can have a conniption over a gerund couldn't possibly have a real life.

She steps back, and Claire and I both walk in.

Under normal circumstances, I would never walk into someone's house without an express invitation, but I am carrying her cookies and I'm also kind of invested in this, or at least it feels like I am.

It feels like I need to see this through 'til the end.

However, the moment I step through the door, I wonder if maybe I should wait outside. A girl, I assume it's Melody, is standing at the stove, her back to us, and she seems to be using a cloth to dab at some kind of white stuff—maybe baking soda?—on the stove.

This is fine, until she turns around, and I realize her entire face and hair are covered in white powder, except for the tear tracks streaked down her face.

"Mom! Oh, Mom!" She throws the rag down and flies to her mother's arms. I wouldn't have been surprised to see her jump up and considering Claire's height—a serious consideration—completely over her mother.

She doesn't. But there is a bit of a thump as the girl crashes into her, making Claire stumble back at least three steps. I almost reach a hand out to steady them, but I'm conscious of my stranger status and the fact that Claire and I didn't exactly hit it off this evening, and of course, there are the cookies in my hand. So I don't.

I stand there awkwardly for what feels like forever, still holding the cookies and watching as Midget trots through the kitchen, sniffs everything, then wanders into the living room.

She lies down. Poor thing. She's been through a lot this evening and is probably ready for a nap.

Another girl, taller than the first one, walks into the kitchen, completely unconcerned with what feels like the catastrophe that has happened, and the wailing coming from who I assume is her sister, and the murmuring of both Tammy and Claire, and is nonchalantly— and, I have to add, quite adeptly—bouncing a basketball, one of those little mini ones, as she walks out. She's got great ball control, manages to miss the doorstop and the doorframe, and continues to bounce as she walks through the tight kitchen.

Even when I was in high school, I didn't have ball control like that. Plus, she's bouncing with her left hand.

I thought Claire's daughter was too young to be on the varsity team. I'm kind of hoping that this is not Claire's daughter but one of the members of the high school girl's squad. If this is the kind of talent they've got on the team, we are definitely looking at a state championship.

This year, no doubt.

It's hard not to get excited about that.

Even while the rational side of my brain says that it's probably Claire's other daughter. I've heard she has two.

Still, maybe Claire's a better coach than I've been giving her credit for if that's what her daughter can do.

Beside me, the girl that Claire is holding pulls back. "I'm so sorry, Mom. I really was paying attention. I know sometimes I have trouble remembering to watch what I'm doing, but I didn't have a book anywhere near the stove. And I wasn't doing any experiments on the side either. I promise."

Claire nodded. "I believe you. Sometimes, even when we're paying attention and trying our hardest, these things happen." She touches her daughter's shoulder. A gentle gesture and such a compassionate one that I almost move closer.

My parents were not as understanding as Claire is being. If they had come home and there had been smoke pouring out the door from me cooking in the kitchen, they would have yelled at me first and talked about it later.

I have to say the lady has impressed me. I feel like this parenting style is much better than the one I grew up under.

I admire her calmness. Toward her child, especially, since I know that not five minutes ago, she was panicking as much as you would expect someone to panic who thought their house was burning down.

"Thanks." The girl's head goes down. "I was browning hamburger. Maybe I had it turned up too high?" Her eyes hold a little question and some apprehension, like maybe that makes everything her fault.

But Claire just smiles, nods, and says, "Go on."

"I stirred it a little bit too vigorously, I guess. Some of the hamburger fell out. It fell down in between the burners. I guess....I guess I should have turned a burner off and picked it out?"

Claire nods again.

"But I didn't. I...I just kept cooking. And moved the skillet so that it was more centered on the burner, so that if any more meat fell out, it would fall out to the side where I could pick it up. I didn't know that was going to catch on fire. Honest!"

So I guess at this point, I realize the Good Grief fire alarm has been going off for a while. But amongst all the chaos in the house, and my relief that the house really wasn't burning down, and my shock to see the type of ballhandling that I witnessed from what looked like a fifteen- or sixteen-year-old, then all of the high school crush feelings that had come back as I walked beside Claire, I guess I didn't register it.

But there is no mistaking the siren, the loudness, and the fact that there is a blinking red light twirling around the walls of the kitchen.

A fire truck pulls in the back drive, parking directly behind Claire's car. I move with Claire and Tammy and Melody and the other little girl toward the door.

I don't know what the fire people are thinking as they jump out of their trucks and see all of us standing at the door.

One white head bobs around the rest and bounces up and down as she jogs down the path and up the stairs.

"Is everyone okay? I assume the fire is out?" I recognize Claire's mother, Mrs. Harding, who hasn't changed a bit in the fifteen years since I'd seen her. Her hair is short and curled around her head, and it is still as white as snow and cut the same way.

She is exactly the kind of no-nonsense person you want in a pinch or an emergency.

Honestly, she is the perfect fire chief.

"It's out, Mom. I'm sorry. I called 911 and never thought to call them back and cancel it."

"We come anyway," her mom said, answering Tammy with a glance.

Her hand reaches out, touching Tammy's cheek, then Melody's

cheek and Claire's cheek and the other little girl's cheek. Her fingers freeze a couple of inches away from mine, and her eyes narrow.

"Who are you?"

I've never seen Mrs. Harding angry, not in all the years I lived beside them. But I wouldn't want to, either. She looks like the kind of woman that wouldn't be afraid to have the live bullet in the firing squad.

"Mom, this is Trey Haywood. Remember him? He lived next door to us all throughout high school."

Claire spoke up, and I notice she didn't mention my basketball accomplishments, which is pretty much what everyone remembers me for.

She also does not mention that she babysat me, which is something her mom would probably remember, too.

"You babysat him," Mrs. Harding says, the hand that had been reaching out to touch my cheek and gather me in like one of her little lambs now tapping her chin. "I remember. I didn't recognize you, son."

She added that "son," and despite the fact that she doesn't touch me, I almost feel like I am part of her lambs.

My mama died when I was still in school, and while Mrs. Harding isn't exactly the traditional mothering type, she does have a way of making a person feel like she will protect her kids no matter what. And maybe they aren't exactly tucked under her wings, but maybe more like protected in her den. Regardless, she makes me miss my mom, giving me that empty longing feeling in my chest that I haven't felt in years.

I thought I was over it.

I guess you never really get over your parent's death.

Maybe that's why I was so quick to run back to Idaho when Dad had a stroke.

Maybe I want to distract myself a little, from the thoughts of my mom and the feelings I had thought I'd gotten over, but while they are chatting, Melody trying to get her story out to her grandmother amid the intermittent hugs that Claire keeps giving her—obviously, now that the fear has worn off, gratefulness that her daughter is alive and unharmed has set in—I turn to the other daughter.

She's stopped bouncing the ball and holds it under her arm pressed against her side. She is chewing gum with her mouth open, snapping it with every other chomp.

Her hair is maybe a shade lighter than Claire's and is pulled straight back in a ponytail. Her face looks young, and now that the two girls are close together, I can see this one is definitely the taller one.

I am curious.

I hold my hand out. "I'm Trey Haywood, your neighbor."

The girl snaps her gum, looking at my hand.

I know a little of how she feels probably. When I was that age, it was always a shock if an adult would hold their hand out to me and treat me like I wasn't a kid.

It doesn't surprise me that it takes her a few moments to pull the ball out from beneath her right arm, shove it under her left, and take my hand.

"I'm Evie. And I knew who you were. We saw you when you moved in." She snaps her gum a few times and looks me up and down. Not in a disrespectful or arrogant kind of way, just in the kind of way a kid does when she's not afraid of you.

She is confident and has nothing to hide. I like her right away.

"Looks like you like to play basketball." I state the obvious and feel like an idiot, but I have to start the conversation somewhere. "You probably love that your mom's the coach."

She blows a bubble while I am talking and waits until it pops before she replies. "I'm too young to play on Mom's team. I mean, they let me play a little, since there's no rule saying I can't, but Mom says she has to be careful because she doesn't want the other girls to get upset. Or their parents."

The girl doesn't roll her eyes or act like this is ridiculous. She kinda acts like it is matter-of-fact. Like it's perfectly okay to not play to keep other people happy.

"How old are you?"

Snap. "Thirteen." She lifts a skinny shoulder, speaking again before I could respond to that. I am surprised. "I know. I don't look like I'm thirteen. That's what everybody says. Mom says it's because I'm so tall. My dad is tall."

Of course. Claire has…had…a husband. Why did that knowledge hit me like a gutshot?

Obviously, she had a husband. She had children. I know this, and yet, it takes me three or four minutes to compose myself and gather my scattered thoughts.

"You're right. I did think you were older. Your mom coaches the varsity team." I know this, but I'm still trying to figure out where Evie fits in.

The varsity team would start with kids in ninth grade. They'd be fourteen or fifteen.

"That's right. And I'm supposed to be on the junior high team, because I'm only in seventh grade, but I'm good enough to play with the older girls, and Mom says there aren't any rules against it, so they let me. I just don't get to play a whole lot."

"Because the other girls are better than you?" That seems like the natural assumption, but her statement from earlier bothers me.

"I don't think so." Evie shrugs her shoulders. "I'm pretty much as good as they are. Better than some. That's what everyone says anyway."

"Then why don't you play? Because you're too young?"

"No. I told you. So the other girls don't get upset. That and their parents." Evie blows another bubble, apparently unconcerned and totally ignorant to the fact that her statement is just bizarre.

When you have a basketball team, you play the best players. You don't not play one so that other people won't get upset.

I keep this to myself. But I figure that is something that will change this year. Although I don't tell her that.

"I bet you're excited for practice to start," I say, wanting to ask about her mother but unsure where Claire's husband fits in the picture, so I don't.

"It's a few months away. It won't start until November. But sometimes, I go to school with Aunt Tammy who goes early, because she's a teacher. I can use the gym until it's time for the other kids to come. I like that."

I figured she did. As good as she is at handling the ball, it is obvious even if she is naturally talented, she still spends time practicing. Even with talent, being good takes hard work.

"I'm trying to talk your mom into starting early." That sounded diplomatic. I am going to insist—no, demand—that basketball practice start sooner rather than later. But that isn't a fight that Evie needs to be in.

My ex complained that I didn't know anything about kids, and she was pretty much right. But I did know when adults disagreed, it wasn't right to have kids in the middle of it.

And I am definitely in a disagreement with Claire if we don't start basketball practice right away.

I hear Claire talking to her mom, apologizing again for getting the whole fire company out for nothing, and so, feeling a pinch of guilt as I do it, I look at Evie and say, "So your dad must be at work?"

"Probably. We don't see him much. He moved to Salt Lake City with his girlfriend or," she snaps her gum a couple of times, "maybe she's his wife now. Mom doesn't usually talk about it. And we're supposed to go to his house over the summer, but we usually don't."

Oh yeah. My lungs feel like they are working properly again. Evie has no idea that she's said everything I want to hear.

I had no idea I wanted to hear it. Not until she says it, and everything settles back down in my chest with the rightness that feels even better than it had before.

Which is crazy, because for most of the time I've spent with Claire, I wasn't even sure I liked her.

But for the entire time, I'd known I was attracted to her. I also haven't had any trouble remembering the crazy hard crush I had on her in high school.

I wasn't the first high school kid to crush on a college girl though.

"You're coming to the dinner at the fire hall tomorrow, right, Trey?" Mrs. Harding's voice cuts through my thoughts.

"Um...I guess. I hadn't realized there was going to be a dinner." It is all I can think of to say. I suppose there's no reason not to go.

"It'll be a nice way for you to reacquaint yourself with everyone in town. Not to mention you'll be supporting a good cause." Mrs.

Harding is a hard woman to say no to, and even though I'm not too interested in going to the fire hall for dinner, I know she is right. Everyone in town will be there.

Somehow with that thought, my eyes land on Claire. She is looking at me, and our eyes meet for a few seconds before she looks away.

I kind of feel like maybe she wants me to go.

"As long as my dad can make it, I'll be there," I hear myself say, and while I am speaking to Mrs. Harding, my eyes slip over to Claire again.

I don't miss the way her lips turn up. It makes me look forward to tomorrow night.

nine

. . .

Claire

IT IS ALWAYS hot in the hall.

I have my hair pulled back in a tight ponytail to keep it out of the spaghetti that I am serving up on people's plates as they come through the line, but a few strands have escaped, and I brush them out of my face.

Sometimes, I think it would be nice to have a buzz cut. I wouldn't have to worry about my hair anymore.

Worry about my hair sure got me into a mess yesterday. I am still embarrassed over that, but at least Trey and I kinda talked about it, and he seemed to understand.

He even admitted to a weakness of his own, which shocked me.

And impressed me.

My ex was always right. Always perfect. Everything he did was always the right thing, and if anything went wrong, it was always my fault.

I hated that.

Me getting blamed for everything.

I hated standing up to him, because then it was a fight, and I hated fighting.

Maybe that's why I always emphasize teamwork and consideration and putting others first in our basketball practices. I really like the way the character of the team has been shaping up over the years since I started.

We are not out to win at any cost. We are out to love each other and lift each other up.

Maybe I couldn't save my marriage, but I can't help but wish that someone had taught my husband these lessons. Maybe being married to him wouldn't have been such a trial.

Maybe he wouldn't have looked at me and seen someone who wasn't as good as he was and wouldn't have decided that he needed to find someone else to fit the perfect picture in his head of who he was and who he needed to complement him.

I slap the spaghetti on the plate that is held out to me, smile, and make an appropriate comment about the weather, shoving those feelings of inadequacy aside.

Even though I know my husband was a jerk, and even though I know for a fact that it isn't my fault that our marriage didn't work, and even though I know the things he told me—that I wasn't good enough, I wasn't young enough, I wasn't what he wanted, and he didn't love me anymore—all show a lack of character on his part and not mine... despite knowing that, it's all head knowledge.

There is a part of me that believes him.

There is a part of me that feels validated, because I had believed all those things all along. I wasn't good enough. When he said it, I believed it, because it's what I had thought.

Even though I know it isn't true, those thoughts still have the power to take me to a place I don't want to go.

"Are you going to answer me? Or are you going to stand there and stare off into space?"

Jerking my head out of the clouds as the words pierce my consciousness, I see Trey standing in front of me with his plate out.

"Sorry."

The man already thinks I am an idiot ditz and a clumsy oaf. Now he knows I am a daydreamer too.

At least that one is true.

Although usually I am dreaming up science experiments to do with my girls. Or thinking about my patients and different ways to try to convince them to do the things—like change their diets—that I know would save their lives.

Sometimes, things just need to be framed in the right way to hit people the way they need to in order to get them interested in changing.

"I'm sorry. I wasn't paying attention. Would you say that again, please?"

He grins a little, almost as though he thinks I'm cute. Which, considering I am over forty, I am officially never going to be cute again in my life.

Still, it is a smile that probably has been devastating to many, and it certainly makes my stomach twist and turn and yawn and stretch and kind of bask in the sunshine that lights up everything on my insides.

"I asked if you were going to be serving all night, or if I could save you a seat and we could talk a little."

"You can save me a seat. Once the line's through, I can go sit down." There will be people who are eating now and will take over serving. It is about that time. We always do it that way, so everyone gets a chance to eat.

"I'll do that." He says it with a finality that makes my stretching stomach pause then narrow and seize. He probably wants to talk about basketball and starting practices.

I've already told him he can. So I don't know why he's talking in that tone of voice.

He waves his plate around, and I realize I never put any spaghetti on it. Digging in, I get a big scoop and slap it on his plate. He looks like the kind of guy who doesn't eat pasta, and I kind of laugh to myself.

Right away, I feel guilty. I am definitely judging him by his looks; there is nothing wrong with cutting out carbs.

I have mostly done it for myself and my kids anyway.

But we don't get legalistic about it.

Like tonight, we are going to eat spaghetti and not think another thing about it.

It isn't going to hurt to eat it once in a while.

It isn't five minutes later when Rosalynn Atwood comes and takes my place in the serving line.

Typically, I eat with Tammy, Leah, and Kori. My girls are off at the corner table they always share with their friends, and my sisters all sitting together, waiting on me. I know they're going to be talking to me later as I walk to the opposite end of the hall and sit down in the chair across from Trey.

His dad, who happens to be one of my patients, is sitting beside him. I nod and greet him.

Interestingly, Lila Bogart, who owns the laundromat and also the small theater in Good Grief, sits across from Trey's dad.

They are about the same age, although I've never seen them together before.

Trey's dad, Clifford, is a nice man, and as far as I know, he's not dated since the death of his wife.

Maybe the stroke has convinced him that he'd rather live than die.

Clifford and Lila are deep in a discussion about the newest play that is going to be opening at the little theater. It sounds like Lila is trying to convince Clifford to be in it.

I hope she is able to because it would be good for him to get out and involved in the community.

He works as a truck dispatcher for a logging company just a little north of town, and as far as I know, that is all he does.

Maybe Lila will convince him to get out and around more.

"I wasn't expecting the spaghetti to be so good. And the salad's not bad either."

"You sound surprised," I say as I unwrap my silverware and pull out my fork.

I hate eating spaghetti in front of people. I never know how to do it. In restaurants, they always serve it with a spoon, which baffles me.

"You have to admit sometimes when people are making food in bulk, quality suffers in favor of quantity. I'm honestly impressed that it didn't."

"Go ahead. You can say it. It's a small town, and your taste buds are spoiled by the elite food of Seattle." I fiddle with my fork, trying to put off the inevitable mess that I'm going to make.

I think I might have mentioned I am klutzy.

I am a sloppy eater as well. My ex pointed that out a time or ten thousand. I am kind of self-conscious about it.

"I wasn't gonna say any such thing." He puts a bite of the salad in his mouth and lifts a brow at me. I guess I should be paying more attention to our conversation, but I notice that his spaghetti is already gone, and I think that's a shame, because if we are both eating spaghetti, then maybe he would be focused on not making a mess out of his, and he wouldn't notice that I am making a mess out of mine.

I suppose this is one of the things I just need to grow up about.

Tempted to cut it up into tiny pieces so I could use my spoon to just scoop it up, I decide to be as adult as I can about it and start trying to get a small enough amount on my fork so I can wind it up and still fit it in my mouth.

"You were. And that's okay. I'm sure there are lots of great restaurants in Seattle."

"Haven't you ever been there?"

"Nope. I've been as far as Boise. And we've vacationed a couple times in Coeur d'Alene. But I've never been to Seattle."

"Never saw the ocean?"

Now I feel like a hick. But I shake my head. It's the honest answer.

I see the look that crosses his face, and I feel even worse.

And then I give myself a mental shake. Who cares? Does it matter? It can't possibly matter what this man thinks of me. Why am I so worried about it?

So I make a decision. Pulling my shoulders back, I look him in the eye. "I don't have a clue how to eat spaghetti properly. They always give you a spoon in the restaurant, and I have never figured out what it's for. I suppose, being that you've lived in Seattle for so long, you know the proper way to eat spaghetti. Care to share?"

I find, after I'm done speaking, that it wasn't as hard as I thought. After all, I just figured out that it doesn't matter what he thinks of me. So what if he thinks I'm a hick because I don't know how to eat spaghetti? And hey, admitting it might mean that I get to find out what that spoon is actually for. One of life's big mysteries solved.

He grins, and I don't get the feeling he is looking down on me.

"Sure. I have to admit I used to wonder the same thing." He holds his hand out for my silverware. "Give it to me, I'll show you."

I hand it over to him, and for some reason, we share a smile. This is probably not the weirdest thing I've ever done, but it's definitely up there. Still, I think it's kind of neat.

I look back down, because I truly do want to know, and my eyes catch on his fingers. They're long, with a bone length and thickness that mark them as a man's, and a slightly paler color that says he works inside, at a desk job.

I like the way they move.

I like the way they look, too. Funny how hands say so much about a person. And his are sure and full of character, with a dexterity I admire.

Man. That stupid crush coming back to haunt me that makes me the kind of person who can wax eloquent about a man's hands. They're not supposed to look that good. I'm definitely not supposed to be making googly eyes over his fingers as he shows me how to eat spaghetti.

He presses the tines of the fork against the spoon, and the light dawns in my head.

"That makes so much sense."

"That's exactly what I thought when I first saw it. Like, duh. I should have known."

I never like to compare, but my ex would have taken that opportunity to rub in that he knew something that I didn't and to make sure I knew exactly how stupid I was.

Maybe, just maybe, I lost a little piece of my heart right there, when he commiserated with me instead of lording it over me. I know there are men like that; I just hadn't been married to one.

"I think you've got it," he says, offering me my utensils back and letting me know by the expression on his face that we are equals, even though he was the one teaching me.

"Thank you," I say. My voice sounds soft, and my heart feels softer.

I'm sure I won't get it right away, and so, to take his attention off my clumsy attempts, I say, "I assume you saved me a seat because you wanted to talk to me?"

"That's right. I was hoping we could discuss the school team and the practice schedule that we're going to have this year. I can speak to the principal again and see what's on the calendar, since I'm sure they already have the game schedule set up."

"I'm sure they do. We can make practices whenever we want to. I've always made up the schedule and turned it in to the office. They make sure it's announced over the loudspeaker and the kids know about it. Nothing much has changed since we went to school. Things are pretty relaxed." I don't need to say small-town Idaho nor comment that it's probably a lot different than the Seattle schools that he'd been used to with his children. He knows that.

And somehow, I feel, like with the spaghetti, he's not going to be a jerk to work with. I'm happy about this, sure. But I'm also worried about my heart. He already has a piece of it. I can't afford to let him have any more.

ten

. . .

Trey

"I KNOW HOW THAT GOES," I say, replying to Claire's comment about the school. It's exactly what I'd expect of my hometown, and it's comforting to know some things haven't changed in the years I've been gone. Even as I speak, I'm thinking. I didn't handle our last conversation very well. Maybe I can do better with this. "I get that you probably weren't planning on starting practices this soon."

"I wasn't," Claire says, holding a small forkful of spaghetti in front of her mouth and speaking before I can draw breath.

Her fast answer makes it sound like she isn't open to change. Hopefully, I can circumnavigate that.

"I understand. You're busy. I'm willing to do all of the practices myself until you're ready to step in. Mostly conditioning things. Some skill work. Legwork, for defense, and a review of positions and their expectations. Maybe some shooting drills and techniques." In my experience, once they reach varsity age, it is difficult to correct bad form, especially when it comes to shooting.

Claire chews while I speak, and I think maybe the look on her face is thoughtful. Hope rises in my chest, but she says, "I don't want the girls to be confused about who's in charge. If you start out leading the practices, and I step in six or eight weeks later, they might continue to look at you as the leader of the team."

I admire her for saying that straight out. It is an honest answer and one that could easily be taken wrong. Like she needs to be in charge, and she isn't giving that up. But that isn't the impression I get. I feel like she truly doesn't want the girls to be confused.

"I get that. I can make sure that I tell them that I'm only stepping in because you allowed and make sure that they understand where my place is." Being an only child, I know I have a rather controlling personality.

When my wife and I were trying to work out our marriage, and then after it blew up, I'd gone to enough counseling sessions to know I have areas I need to work on. And I have worked on those areas. It didn't save my marriage, but I do think that maybe I have become at least a slightly better person.

That was years ago, but I haven't forgotten the lessons. Mostly because the ones that resonate the most with me are the ones I'd learned in Sunday school growing up anyway. Sometimes, we just think we have a better idea.

Or forget the things we've been taught.

"I think whenever we start practices, we ought to be there together." Again, Claire isn't coming off in a commanding way, and I think she's making an effort to make the best of a situation that she isn't necessarily completely happy with.

It was probably a shock for her to find out that she was going to have an assistant coach after years of doing it all herself.

"That's fine with me. I do think we need to start practicing though. The girls didn't win a single game last year." I put a hand up. "I'm not blaming you. But I think there's enough talent on the team," I think of her daughter Evie's ballhandling, "that we should be able to do at least a little better."

"Winning isn't everything."

"But it would encourage the girls. It might not be everything, but it's a natural goal when you're playing a game to play to win."

I would never call Claire stubborn. Studious and smart, yes. Funny, and even quirky, after living beside her. And honestly, there was still that schoolboy crush that makes me not exactly fear her, but definitely respect her, and feel like she was a little untouchable.

Yeah, maybe I hold her on a pedestal some.

But I also want to do a good job on this basketball team. I'm not going to go back to Seattle and admit that I helped coach a team that went oh for fifteen again.

"So it'll take a week at least to give the girls notice that we're starting practice. And for everyone who wants to join the team to get physicals. I say we start practice in two weeks. That would be the beginning of October."

This is a huge compromise from Claire. She isn't even suggesting we start halfway between when I want to start, which is now, and when she wants to start, which is the middle of November.

I certainly am not going to turn it down.

"Thank you. I appreciate the fact that you aren't demanding to even meet in the middle. You are giving more. Thank you."

"This is part of what I'm teaching the girls. I want them to learn that it's okay to not get your way all the time. However, I do think since I'm the head coach, I should run the practices."

That definitely puts a pinprick in my elation, but the air in my chest oozes out slowly. Even if she does run the practices, I surely will be able to get a group of girls each time and work with them myself.

I have visions of the team having a winning record this year. If not winning the championship.

I feel like the conversation is a win. For me.

eleven

. . .

Claire

"BUT, Mom, I'm ten. I'm old enough to be home by myself. I shouldn't have to sit through basketball practice. I'm wasting my life." Melody hugs her books to her chest, her backpack slung over her shoulder, as she repeats the argument that she's been using on me for the last two weeks, ever since I told her basketball practice is starting at the beginning of October and she will have to wait to go home from school until I am done with it each evening.

"I know you're more than old enough to be home by yourself. But I just feel safer if you're here."

"Mom, you have to let go sometime."

"You're right. But not today."

"Mom, you're treating me like a baby."

"I'm not. I'm just playing it safe. You'll thank me someday."

"I'll thank you for treating me like a two-year-old when I'm ten?" Melody's eyes narrow, and she gives me a look that feels so familiar her father could be standing in front of me instead of her. "I don't think so."

I think she knows I'm not changing my mind, because she huffs, then stomps away to the bleachers where she slams her bookbag down and plops down on the seat, tilting her body so her shoulder faces me.

I don't smile, although I am tempted to.

Originally, I had truly planned that she could go home and be by herself. Last year, I'd almost allowed it, because she is so responsible, and lots of people leave their kids home alone.

But two things stop me.

The first is her father. I know if anything happens to my children, he has the money and connections to hire a lawyer and take them from me. Not that he's ever seemed inclined to do so, but he did give me a hard time two summers ago when Evie broke her wrist. She'd been riding her bike right in front of me, and the next thing I knew, she was on the ground screaming.

It wasn't a bad break, and it healed with no complications, but Cody acted like I was negligent and the most horrible parent in the world.

The second reason is the night she almost burned the house down. Of course, that is an exaggeration.

There'd been a small fire on the stove, which had been contained quickly and easily.

But it scared me. It could have been so much more so fast, and I could have lost her.

I still haven't recovered fully from it. And that is the other reason that I just can't leave her home by herself.

Call me a helicopter mom. Or overprotective. I'd rather have labels and names than a dead daughter.

Plus, the things I am going to do with the team are things I want Melody to participate in anyway.

Trey hasn't arrived, and that doesn't surprise me. He already told me that he'd probably be a little late, since he'd be taking off early from work to make it.

I already have things worked out with my job where I work eight to two every day and make up the hours by spending one night a week with a patient that needs round-the-clock care.

That way, I am there for my girls before school and after school, and they have a special night with Tammy every week. It's worked out pretty well.

I walk over toward where the girls are huddled around the basket.

The only one with the ball is Evie who is dribbling and occasionally taking a shot. I'm not sure where she gets her talent and love of basketball, since neither Cody nor I are interested in the sport, but she definitely gets her height from her father, and somehow, she picked up a ball when she was little—I don't even remember what age because I thought it was just a passing fancy—started dribbling and shooting, and slowly started getting better.

When I tell the girls to line up, she is standing on the three-point line. She turns and tosses the ball without really seeming to take aim. It swishes through—all net—then she jogs over to where the girls are gathered at the foul line.

"Show-off," Rachel says, with a smile that only has a little bit of sneering in it.

That's part of the reason I don't let Evie play any more than what I have. I'm not exactly an expert in basketball, but she is better than any of the girls on the team.

It looks like this year we are going to have—I count heads—four girls, including Evie.

We had six last year, but three of them were seniors, so four isn't too bad.

Evie doesn't respond to Rachel, and she wouldn't. Evie has such an easygoing personality. I don't know if I've ever seen her upset or offended.

"I'm so glad to see everyone here," I begin. "I hope we have a good time this year and learn to be kind people who think of others." I go on to talk about Trey and explain that he'll be the assistant coach.

Everyone already knows it. It's been two weeks since it was decided, and Good Grief is a small town. Still, I feel like it's my job.

I finish up and look around the small group, asking if there are any questions.

The girls shake their heads as footsteps echo on the gym floor—a long stride—and I assume that's probably Trey.

Perfect timing. I smile at the girls.

"And as tradition demands, we'll use the first basketball practice to pick up trash around the school."

twelve

. . .

Trey

I CAN'T HELP IT. I screech to a stop. She's going to have the girls do what for basketball practice?

I've been telling myself for two weeks I will let her lead, and I will guide the practices in the direction I want them to go, not by butting heads with her but by gently steering things in the direction of my preferences, possibly working with small groups and showing her that building on a foundation, conditioning, and putting the work in at the beginning of the season is the way a person builds a winning basketball team.

I realize, as I listen to Claire's voice die away, that I have underestimated the pickle I have gotten myself into.

I have also completely misconstrued Claire's plans for the season.

Thinking back, I know she said exactly what she planned to do—build character in the girls—and I had totally put my spin on what she was saying and assumed that she meant she was going to build character through basketball.

I am just starting to understand that what she actually meant was she planned to use the time that was set aside for basketball practice to do things that will build character, things that have absolutely nothing whatsoever to *do* with basketball.

76

Even if she had sent the girls to go take a three-mile run, she would have at least been facing in the right direction.

As it is, going out to pick up garbage, she isn't facing in the right direction, she isn't even... I don't even know. She isn't even on the planet. It's like she is out on Jupiter, looking toward Pluto.

I can't allow this. We are only having two practices per week until the season starts. We can't waste them going out picking up trash.

I stomp over, determined to fix this and lay down a few ground rules right away. I need to start the way I intend to go on.

And while I admire Claire for wanting to teach the girls character and have nothing personally against picking up trash, it isn't what basketball practice is for.

I form my argument in my head as I walk over, and even though I'm steaming, I'm not so upset that I can't say what needs to be said calmly and rationally.

I stop beside her, my mouth opens, and she turns.

Those eyes, the green emeralds that I always have trouble looking away from, sparkle with life and happiness, and I can see the joy and affection she has for every girl there and the excitement caused by making a difference in their lives—it's all on her face. In her eyes. I see it, even with my mouth open and the words that I feel need to be said trembling inside my lips.

"I'm so glad you made it before we dispersed." She smiles at me, the same smile that she shot me across the table when I'd shown her how to use her spoon with her spaghetti. One that thanks me and appreciates that I don't make fun of her, and one that makes me feel like I'm part of her inner circle, welcome and appreciated.

I sigh to myself, putting my hands in my dress slacks pockets.

My idea of a good coach is one who is always dressed for the occasion.

I'm not dressed to pick up trash.

I am dressed to coach basketball.

She seems to realize this as her eyes slide down to my tie. They take in my dress pants and the shoes, which mark me clearly as a nonlocal, even though I am.

A local would be wearing cowboy boots.

Her eyes slide back up to mine, and she says, "I'm sorry. I guess I should have told you what I was planning for today."

She doesn't need to tell me I'm not dressed for her unconventional activity. I know it.

She turns back to the girls. "I told you Mr. Haywood would be the assistant coach this year, and I'd like to introduce you all to him."

She starts with a girl named Rachel, the tallest girl on the team aside from Evie, who stands on the opposite end and is introduced last.

When I first walked in, I'd noticed how small the group was. I had assumed this was just the seniors or maybe the new players, but... "This is the whole team?" I ask and try not to look as horrified as I feel.

Claire nods, smiling, and I don't think she has a clue that my heart just dropped to my toes, cowboy boots or no.

Four kids? There are four girls on the team total?

Good Grief is a small school, sure, but at least when I played back in the day, we never had trouble filling the team.

Four girls didn't even make a full team.

"Is there any chance that other girls will join closer to time for the season?" I ask, hoping that there is something going on, some sickness sweeping the school, play practice that is interfering with basketball, alien abduction, anything that is keeping us from having all the girls here today.

But I've barely gotten the sentence out before Claire shakes her head.

"This is actually one more than I was expecting. I hadn't been sure that Kenzie was going to make it." She shoots a grin at the blonde-haired girl who smiles back, showing teeth with a set of hardware that would set off metal detectors.

At least the girls seem to really love Claire.

Part of me thinks they must really love something if they are willing to stay after school and pick up garbage and call it basketball practice.

Maybe they just have bad home lives.

Pain, unexpected and sharp, shoots through me, and for the second time since I've moved to Good Grief, I have that empty, cold feeling in my chest and wish I could talk to my mother.

She was always sociable and up on everything. She would know about the home lives of the girls right off and be able to tell me if anything needed to be done about them.

"All right then, let's go outside and get started. Evie, you can grab the bags out of my car." Claire claps her hands together, and the girls grin, three of them giggling amongst themselves while Evie walks a little ways off, not quite part of the group.

Going through high school, I'd never really had that problem, not more than a time or two, where I didn't feel like I fit in. I had plenty of friends backing me, thanks to my skill in basketball.

Somehow, when a kid stands out as a sports figure, lots of people decide they like you, no matter what kind of person you are. I didn't always like the people I hung out with, but I always had people *to* hang out with.

Still, there were one or two times I remember where I felt like I was on the outside looking in.

It isn't a good feeling, and I feel a little bad for Evie, who obviously loves basketball but really isn't being given the opportunities or even the attention she deserves.

I try not to think about that too much though. Honestly, from what I've seen in my life, the harder someone has it, the more they have to overcome, the better they eventually do. It's like adversity makes them stronger.

It makes sense, and I believe it to be true, but it's still hard to watch.

I take my eyes from the girls' retreating backs and look at Claire, who has gone over to pick up the basketball that sits in the corner.

"So is this like a tradition that you do at the beginning of every season?" I am pretty sure it has to be.

As much as I hate to waste even one practice, I can wait until Thursday to get started with my plans.

Claire bends down and picks up the ball, holding it in front of her with her hands positioned the way a pregnant woman might position her hands around her belly. "It is. We pretty much use the first practice to clean up the school. I think it teaches the girls to take pride in their facilities and also reminds them, of course, that if you throw garbage down, somebody has to pick it up."

"Yeah. I see that you're making sure you're teaching good lessons in character for the girls." I want to say more, like they could learn some lessons through basketball, but I don't because she starts again.

"That's right. I'm glad that we see the same thing. I was worried that you were going to be all 'we gotta do drills and run and do all the boring stuff that sucks the joy out of their life,' and really, there's no point to that anyway." She smiles as though her words hadn't just struck me in the middle of my forehead.

All the stuff she just mentioned was exactly what I want to do.

Only, it isn't pointless.

"So you start on all that other stuff in the second practice?" I couldn't bring myself to say "pointless stuff."

"No, we never do that garbage. There's always something that actually has meaning to it that needs to be done. Someone that needs help. Places that can use willing hands and happy smiles." Honestly, my pulse is throbbing in my forehead, but I'm also admiring how Claire glows and becomes animated with excitement as she waves an arm and her cheeks turn pink. "We can bring life and light to so many people, and that's what I always use the basketball practices for. It's just a waste of time to throw a ball around and try to get it into a hoop. What's the point of that anyway?" She sets the ball in the rack along with three other balls, all of which look flat to me, which probably states just how important basketballs are to the girls on the school team and also that Evie either blew that ball up herself or was smart enough to pick the only one that had air in it.

I am betting it was the first.

As long as I keep my focus on the balls and think about Evie blowing one up in order to dribble it and shoot a hoop or two and take deep breaths through my nose, I keep myself from screaming like I want to.

Maybe not screaming. Yelling. Stomping over to Claire and demanding she resign from her position, effective immediately.

Someone who doesn't even see the point of basketball has absolutely no business coaching a team. None.

I could hardly fathom that she is the girls' varsity coach, and she is talking about a sport that I love, one that I excelled at and learned so many great things from, like it is meaningless.

I want to throttle her, grab her by her shoulders and shake her until she sees what I see. Something that gives kids purpose. Something that gives them meaning in life and the skills to go from clumsy to athletic, that will teach them sportsmanship and handling pressure and help develop the character it takes to pick yourself up after a loss, to dig in more, harder, with all the grit and perseverance in your body, to claw your way back to a win, even when, *especially when,* you don't feel like it.

There are so many lessons in the sport of basketball, *so many,* and Claire is dismissing it like it is sugar in a keto diet.

But as upset as I am about her words, I can't be upset with the person herself.

She is doing what she feels is right. She's donating her time and her knowledge to girls who might not—probably don't—appreciate it.

Maybe she is a little discouraged because there aren't more kids out, and maybe she is making the best of things.

I walk slowly toward her, my hands still in my pockets, my mind spinning.

I had no idea things were this bad.

I don't even know where to start.

"Were you expecting more girls?"

"It would be nice to have a few more. I'll have to play Evie now, and there will be some parents who are upset about that. No one will get a break either, and the girls get tired running up and down and all around constantly."

I bite the inside of my cheek and keep my voice level. "If she's good enough to play, she should play. It shouldn't matter what people think."

"I think we've had this discussion before, and it does matter what people think. We want to be careful not to offend anyone."

Being that I lived in Seattle, I feel like I should be the one telling someone from Good Grief that we shouldn't offend people, but Claire has turned the tables on me, and somehow, I am the one who is scrambling for words to explain why we don't need to worry about offending people.

She gives my clothes another glance. "I understand if you don't want to help pick up trash. You're not exactly dressed for it. And I'm sure it's not your favorite pastime anyway." Her voice is nonchalant along with her body language, but as much as I want to accept her offer, I won't.

"I'm the assistant coach. If the basketball team is picking up trash, then that's what I'm doing. Whether I like it or not. Whether I'm dressed for it or not."

Those are the words that come out of my mouth, and that's really how I felt. Part of basketball is the team spirit. You never let your teammates down, not with your actions, not with your playing, not with your mouth or attitude.

Now there is a lesson that builds character.

"I'm happy to hear that." Claire smiles at me, her eyes sparkling. I am close enough to see the emerald green.

Regardless of how much we disagree about basketball, and I'm not even sure she realizes exactly how much we disagree, I'm not going to pass up the opportunity to work with Claire.

thirteen

. . .

Claire

I GO to the gym on Thursday with an apprehension pulling in my chest.

The girls are huddled in their usual spot down by the far basket, with Evie dribbling around the three-point line, occasionally taking shots, and making all of them.

Tuesday's practice went better than I thought it would. I had expected Trey to pitch a fit when he found out that I was having the girls pick up trash.

I assume he didn't think that was the way basketball practice should be run. I am fairly certain he had never been to a basketball practice that had been run like that.

But he surprised me. Pleasantly.

Not only had he not argued with me or even suggested that we do even one thing that he wanted, but he'd rolled up the sleeves on his dress shirt and pitched in picking up the trash.

He had the girls giggling, and maybe ten years ago, they probably all would have had crushes on him.

If I looked at him now through the eyes of my teenage self, I don't think I would have.

Back then, someone in their mid- to late thirties seemed like an old man to me.

His hairline had started to recede, and as he had pointed out to me at Mrs. Thompson's house, he definitely didn't have six-pack abs.

But looking at him through the eyes of my forty-one-year-old self?

I don't care about the hair. I don't care about the abs either.

Hair says nothing about character, and neither do abs.

What I really admire about him is his willingness to continue working with me even though I'm not doing things the way he knows they should be done.

That he is willing to pitch in and help.

That he isn't too good to pick up trash.

That he would actually spend his time with a bunch of ragtag girls who obviously are not going to win again this year either.

I'd heard he'd been offered a head coaching position in the next county—rumor only. I'd also heard he'd turned it down.

Whether it was true or not, he had the freedom to leave, and yet he chose to stay. With me.

And only four girls.

We had six girls last year, and I'd been able to sub girls in throughout the game as they got tired.

This year, they'd have to play the whole game themselves.

I'd learned, after three seasons of coaching, that it is possible to foul out.

None of my girls have ever done that, of course.

I would put them on the bench long before they fouled out.

We follow the rules explicitly, and fouls are not well tolerated by me.

It is more important to be considerate and gracious and kind than it is to have to do anything that requires a potential foul.

I definitely drilled that into their heads the first time one of my girls got three fouls in a game.

That never happened again.

Still, as much as I admire Trey for seeing things my way, as much as I love his kindness and consideration, and even with that little attraction—probably attraction that is left over from high school and college—it isn't enough to make a relationship.

My failed marriage taught me that at least.

A relationship needs to be built on shared values and things you have in common. Trey and I have practically nothing in common. Including basketball. Since we have such differing views on the subject.

Still, I can't deny that my heart beats faster when he is around, and there is a lot about him to admire. Even if we don't agree.

"It's good to see you all today, girls. You did a great job of picking up trash on Tuesday. Thank you."

They chatter a bit while they line up on the foul line.

I spend some time talking with them about school and hobbies and what they are doing, and we joke a little bit.

Then I straighten up and say, "Today, we're heading to the nursing home, where we're going to ride along with the residents as they take a trip to Walmart. Some of them just need someone to walk alongside them while they pick out their purchases, and some of them might have a list to hand you, and they'll expect you to pick out the things on it. Of course, I will be there to help if you have any questions, and I'll be in charge of paying for anything and handling the money. I know you girls will be a big help to ladies that might not be able to walk around the store anymore but still want to make their own purchases."

We've done it before last year, so the two returning team members know what to expect. It's a little bit crazy and a little bit hard because some of the ladies are very picky about wanting the exact kind of item they specify and aren't willing to substitute.

But sometimes, people are difficult to deal with, and we have to continue to be kind and gracious to them anyway. What a great lesson for the girls.

I feel like there is no better place for the girls to learn character than an assisted living center. I am glad my sister Leah is the activities director and that she allows us to do the shopping trip with the residents there.

"You're going to a nursing home today?"

I hadn't heard Trey walk in. I definitely hadn't heard his footsteps across the floor.

I turn and see he's dressed in basketball shorts, a T-shirt that is exactly the right size, and sneakers.

He got along so well with the garbage thing that I hadn't thought about letting him in on what I am doing today.

Once he got used to the idea, it seemed like he hadn't cared. I was sure he was starting to see that I am going to be doing things a little differently.

"Mr. Haywood. I'm so glad you made it," I say, loving that my voice sounds cool and professional.

My insides definitely don't feel that way, at least not the part of me that is still in high school and gets flustered around an attractive man.

Did I mention his t-shirt?

Okay, that seems a little shallow, and honestly, I don't want some man drooling over me because of a t-shirt, but truly, I wouldn't look twice at him if I didn't know the character of the man in the t-shirt. That makes all the difference.

I suppose some of you know what I'm talking about—he looks good to me, physically, because I'm looking at him from the inside out.

Alright, enough grown-up talk.

The man is yummy.

Even the grown-up part of me can appreciate the way he looks striding across the floor as well. I smile bigger than I need to and swallow against the hammering of my heart.

I am so caught up in admiring him that he is almost to me before I realize he asked me a question and way too much silence has elapsed without me answering.

So much for the cool voice.

It's only been a few seconds, and hopefully, the girls haven't noticed that Mr. Haywood has basically rendered me speechless.

I try to give him a professional and cool look. I hope my voice doesn't sound like a high school cheerleader when I say, "We are. Going to a nursing home today. The residents just love to see the girls. And—"

"It builds character. I get it."

He doesn't sound super happy, but maybe he's had a bad day at work. I realize I actually don't know anything about him. Well, nothing about his current life. Like what he actually does for work.

Tomorrow, his dad is on my rotation, and maybe I can get a little information out of him.

I pick up on the subject I think bothers him. "You don't have to go. I mean, of course you're welcome to. But it will probably last longer than a typical ball practice, and I totally understand if you've worked all day, you don't want to spend the rest of your afternoon and evening helping the elderly go shopping."

"Oh. That's what we're doing. Shopping with the elderly."

There's something odd about his tone, and I nod slowly. My smile has slipped, and I know my eyes are slightly narrowed as I tilt my head, trying to figure out what's going on. "Yes."

I almost repeat my offer that he doesn't have to go, but I know he heard me plenty well the first time. Whatever his problem is, it can't be anything that I've done.

Lifting my chin, I turn back to the girls. "All four of you can fit in my car. Make sure you bring your bags and stuff with us, since we won't be stopping back at the school before I drop you off at your houses."

"Should I follow you?"

Trey's tone still doesn't seem quite right, but the look on his face is completely devoid of any emotion, and I stop trying to figure it out.

"You can. We're going to Cherry Tree Assisted Living." I don't need to explain where it is. It's the only assisted living home in our county.

Sure enough, he nods. "I'll try to keep up," he says, and I feel like there's a bit of sarcasm in his voice.

I'm not sure where that's coming from.

I turn and start walking. He falls into step beside me.

"Is it okay if I ask a question?" he asks, and although it feels like that question should make him sound insecure, he actually doesn't.

"Sure. I hope I'm not so intimidating that you're afraid to speak up." I know I'm not.

I'm the least intimidating person on the planet.

"You can be fearsome," he says, and my head jerks sideways, my eyes wide. That has to be a joke.

Trey looks just as serious as he did when we were standing back with the girls.

"You have to be the only person in the world who thinks that way. No one has ever accused me of being scary, or intimidating, or even loud."

Probably if I had been a little bit more assertive, I wouldn't have been married as long as I had been. I really let my ex walk all over me.

I guess staying married had been more important to me than getting my own way.

In the end, it hadn't mattered. He found someone else anyway.

"Maybe I see a side of you that no one else does."

I laugh. "In a way, that's true. You live beside me, so no one else gets the view of my house that you do."

"Where's Melody?" He looks around.

"Is that the question you are free to ask me?" I ask, and I'm not really joking. I'm kind of aghast that he would feel like he needed to ask permission to ask a question like that.

"No. I just realized she's not around. And I thought you'd made her stay the last time because you didn't want her home alone."

"Oh, yeah. My mom and sister had gone to Coeur d'Alene, and there was no one home." I should have made her come, and normally I would have, but she's been working on this big science project, hoping to place well in the local competition and move on to regionals.

"So she's with your sister?"

"Yeah. I'll pick her up on the way home."

"She's not interested in basketball?"

"No. She inherited my propensity for science. I have to watch her pretty closely, or she'll have experiments going on everywhere. Most of the time, they don't explode, but every once in a while…"

"I see. You have to worry about your house burning down."

"We live pretty close to the fire station, and with my mom being the fire chief, that's not typically something I spend a lot of time worrying about, but yes, it could be a concern with Melody."

"I don't recall you ever having a problem growing up."

"My love for science has more of a bent toward biology. Hers definitely veers off toward a lot of chemistry." I hear the pride in my voice, and I try to temper it. Everyone's proud of their kids. No one likes to hear anyone brag about them.

"She's smart." It isn't a question. He is making a statement, and it is really hard for me not to gush.

"I guess."

"False modesty?"

That is a question.

"Guilty." I slip my gaze over at him, and my eyes are crinkled. They match his.

"I'm proud of my boys too. I get it."

"They're with your ex?"

"Yeah."

He doesn't elaborate, and I don't really feel like we know each other well enough for me to probe. Maybe by the end of the season.

"The question I asked permission to ask is…" He clears his throat and slows slightly. The girls, giggling and chatting, walk out of the gym. "Are we ever going to actually practice basketball at basketball practice?"

Now he does sound a little insecure. His hands are clasped behind his back as he walks alongside me, and his shoulders move a little more than what they had been. Maybe it's a tell. A nervous tell.

Although I don't know why he might be nervous asking me about that, unless he really cares about the answer.

"It bothers you?" I ask, answering his question with one of my own, trying to figure out what the issue is.

"Would it make you mad if I say it does bother me some?"

"It won't make me mad. But I don't agree."

"You don't think basketball practice should include basketball?"

"I think there are more important things in life than basketball. And spending a lot of time learning how to play it is a waste. But going to an assisted living home and helping other people is not."

"I can't argue with you about helping people. I think that's a good thing. But I also think it's a good thing to exercise, to learn skills, to have the discipline to keep working at something and get better. There are a lot of lessons to be learned in sports. They're not necessarily completely worthless."

He has me figured out. Because that's exactly how I feel about sports. Completely worthless. For the most part anyway.

I suppose he is kind of right in a lot of ways though. There are lessons a person can learn, and the ones he is talking about are some of the good ones.

I don't want to argue with him, and I really don't have anything planned for Tuesday, so I say, "We'll practice basketball on Tuesday. Does that satisfy you?"

He doesn't need to answer me. His lips have curved up in a contented smile like I handed him a victory.

Maybe I did.

I certainly hadn't been planning on practicing basketball on Tuesday. But if it would make him happy, we could use Tuesday as basketball something or other and then continue to build character in the girls by doing other things on Thursday.

"It does. Thank you."

fourteen

. . .

Trey

I WALK into Lone Pine Tavern and take a seat at the corner table over by the far wall.

It's the only eatery in Good Grief, and yes, it serves alcohol, so it doubles as a bar, but it also has the best fries in the Pacific Northwest and possibly the entire United States.

They're reasonably priced, too.

I place an order of fries, which is big enough to be a meal, and they really don't need ketchup or any condiments, but I like barbecue sauce on them, and a drink, then I lean back in my seat, putting my hand over the bench back, and look out the window.

I hadn't really gotten to spend much time with Claire after we got in our separate cars. We didn't spend much time at the assisted care facility, since Leah had everyone ready for us.

I ended up with three men, and we spent an hour and a half wandering through the sporting goods section of the department store.

None of them ended up buying anything, but they seemed to have a great time just looking.

I actually had a pretty good time watching them and listening to their stories about the hunting and the fishing they'd done over their lives, and one of them had been a bear trapper, and boy, did he have stories to tell. I hadn't even realized people did that for a living.

I suppose spending time with older folk just naturally lends itself to contemplation.

And I wonder what I will be talking about when I am their age.

Their age feels a lot closer now than it did when I was in high school.

I wonder if I will look back on my life and wish I'd done things differently.

That is almost a given. Since I already look back on my life and some mistakes I've made and wish I'd not been stupid.

Of course, there are lessons I learned because of those mistakes, lessons I wouldn't have learned otherwise, and I could hardly resent that.

"Trey Haywood. I'd heard you were back in town. I figured I'd run into you eventually."

I jerk my head away from the window at the familiar voice from my past.

Mr. Woodley, the basketball coach through my high school years, the one who'd coached when we won the state championship and I'd been chosen as an all-state baller.

He and I go way back, and I have the greatest amount of respect for him.

I slide out of the booth and stand up, holding my hand out. "Mr. Woodley. It's great to see you." I look around. There's no one with him.

My brows push together as I try to remember if I've heard anything about his wife.

I know he had one.

They had the team over every year at the end of the season for a big barbecue at their house. It was always winter and freezing cold. We had a huge bonfire, and we'd go sledding and ice skating. It lasted all night and was always a ton of fun. I never really talked to his wife much, but any woman who would have a group of guys over and let them have free range of her home and property, who would cook for them without complaint and make enough desserts to fill two tables, is a good woman in my book.

As we finish our handshake, I say, "Are you here by yourself? Would you like to sit with me?"

A ghost of a cloud passes over Mr. Woodley's eyes, and I wish in a small way that I hadn't said anything. But in another way, I'm glad I did, because he nods.

"I'd love that, son. Mrs. Woodley passed away five years ago, and it gets a little lonely without her. I get tired of my own company, and I get really tired of eating by myself."

A little grin tilts up one side of his mouth, and I remember that look from my basketball years. Mr. Woodley has a great sense of humor, although he pushed us to what we thought were our limits and then beyond. I'll be forever grateful for the lessons he taught me and in particular for the fact that he showed me that I could do a lot more than what I thought I could.

He slides into the seat across from me. "I get even more tired of cooking for myself. It stinks."

"I can relate to that. I'm a terrible cook."

"Your wife died?"

"No. She claimed I was immature and only interested in myself, and she left me for a guy who apparently was better than that."

I guess it is my turn to be a little sad. I suppose I am well over my wife.

A person can kill love really fast with insults and the kinds of degrading comments she hurled at me what felt like nonstop the last year we were together, but I didn't just lose my wife. I lost my family, my boys, the home I thought I'd built, even my cats. It stunk. Especially since I don't even know what I could have done differently to have kept it all.

One side of Mr. Woodley's mouth pulls back, and he nods slowly. "Kids nowadays don't have the grit to work on their marriages. They expect everything to be handed to them, and they walk out when things get hard." He shakes his head. "I know there are two sides to every story, but I wasn't really talking about you."

"I know," I say, even though he could have been. I'm sure I could have done more. The thing was, I was willing to work on it; she just didn't give me a chance.

"But surely there are some happier things we can talk about."

I nod and smile, and then wait while the waitress takes his order and walks away.

We catch up on some of what he's been doing, when he retired, and the cancer that took his wife. I talk about my job in Seattle and how I moved back in with my dad when he had the stroke. I tell him I don't plan on staying, just hanging out long enough to make sure he gets back on his feet and maybe adopts a few healthier habits.

"He's pretty young," Mr. Woodley says.

"Almost sixty," I agree. "He should have lots of good life left, if he'll listen to the doctor."

"Habits are hard to change."

"That's true. But he's pretty motivated. The stroke scared him, and I think he has a lady he's interested in."

"I'd love to see that happen for him. He and your mother were perfect soulmates, and when he lost her, he lost a huge part of himself. It took him a long time to get over that."

I unwrap my straw, studying it very carefully. Giving it much more attention than it needs as I put it in the drink the waitress has just set down.

One of the worst things about coming back to Good Grief is the way the memories that I haven't even thought about in years kind of sneak up on me at the oddest times.

The sadness that I thought I'd put behind me forever twists my heart. I miss my mom. I miss having a mom and dad. I miss the family atmosphere that we created together when I was with them.

"I'm not sure if death is worse than divorce or not. If they were divorced, I would probably just be wishing that they were back together. Forever. I don't think I'd ever give that up."

It's probably the way my boys feel, although I've never talked to them about it. My ex has said a lot of things about me to them—things that aren't true—and when I am with them, I do everything I can to show them that I am not the man she claims I am.

I envy my dad the years he got to spend with his soulmate.

I never had that.

Maybe that is a little of the reason behind the longing for my mom. I just want someone who loves me no matter how bad I screw up. Who sees the best in me, even if there isn't much of that to see, who is willing to give up whatever she needs to see to my happiness.

But even as I'm thinking that, I realize…I was never that for my ex. I never saw only the good in her. I never turned a blind eye to her mistakes and screwups, and I never gave up anything for her happiness. I was too concerned about my own.

But I didn't want to pour my heart and soul into someone who wasn't going to appreciate it. Who was going to take advantage of me.

Maybe that is the risk of love.

Maybe that risk is worth it, because if it works the way it is supposed to, I would end up with a woman who does the same for me —my soulmate.

I like that idea but don't know how to start to reach for the reality it represents.

Mr. Woodley has taken a drink, and now I have to pull myself out of my contemplation as he continues our conversation. "I don't think kids ever do. But at least if your parents were divorced, you'd get to visit your mother."

"But it would be so weird seeing her with another man. It's hard enough to think about my dad and his interest in Mrs. Bogart. I'm happy for him, but it's weird."

"That's what your kids are going to think when they see you dating someone else."

"I know." I don't even bother to deny that I would date someone else.

I want to.

I want the family.

I want the house filled with love and laughter.

I want my soulmate.

Somehow, I think of Claire and her crazy ideas of what basketball practice entails.

Almost as though Mr. Woodley can sense my wandering thoughts, he says, "I heard you're the assistant girls' basketball coach."

There's not the slightest hint of a smile or humor on his face, and I have to deduce that either he doesn't know about Claire and the way she runs her program, or he approves.

Both seem kind of impossible to me.

"Yeah. Claire Harding is the head coach." I try to say that casually. "They had a winless season last year," I add, even though I'm sure he knows it.

"Nowhere to go but up," he says easily. He picks his drink up, taking a sip of his water and setting it back down carefully.

"That's a great attitude." I wish it were that easy. Even one win would be better than last season, but with the way Claire runs things, and with only four girls, I'm not holding out much hope that is going to happen.

"So what's your role?" Mr. Woodley asks casually.

"What do you mean? I'm the assistant coach. I do whatever she tells me to."

"And what has she told you to do?"

"Nothing. I just tagged along while she's..." I look up at Mr. Woodley, and he is staring at me, listening, like he really wants to know what's going on.

"Yeah?" he prompts when I trail off.

"I want to complain about her," I say. And that's really all I intend to say.

"So don't. Just tell me what basketball practice is like. You had what, two?"

He's as connected as I would have thought in this small town.

I twist my drink around and am grateful when the waitress interrupts us, setting my fries and barbecue sauce down in front of me and a salad down in front of Mr. Woodley.

It's what I should have gotten, but it's been so long since I have had their fries I couldn't resist.

He lifts a brow at my fries and then says, "I'll pray for the food."

I nod and bow my head, remembering that back when I was in school, Mr. Woodley prayed in the locker room or on the bus before every game.

I appreciated that.

It made me feel good to think that I was working as hard as I could, and then God was picking up where I left off. It also seemed to my teenage self that God wouldn't be able to say no to Mr. Woodley, where it wouldn't be as hard for Him to say no to me.

Erroneous thinking, now that I am older, but it made me feel good as a teenager.

His prayer isn't long, and he already has his fork picked up when I open my eyes and look back up.

"So, are you gonna tell me about it?"

I grin a little. "I've got a feeling you already know."

"Maybe. But I'd like to hear about it from you." He stabs a few pieces of lettuce and a cherry tomato, lifting them up. "Unless, of course, you don't want to talk about it."

"I would. I'd love some advice. I really don't know what to do."

"Talk away."

So I tell him. I tell him about the fact that originally, she wasn't going to have any basketball practices until the season started.

And then, when I talked her into starting practices now, she uses them as community benevolence.

That there are only four kids on the team. And one of those is a thirteen-year-old.

I end by telling him she promised that there would be actual basketball practice on Tuesday, and throwing a hand up, one with fries and barbecue sauce in it, I say, "I don't know what to do. I don't have the authority to demand we do something, *anything*, that would help the girls play better ball, and…" I pause here because I'm about to say something that I haven't said to anyone. "I don't want to fight with Claire. I like her."

At that admission, which he probably knows I didn't intend to make, Mr. Woodley smiles.

"You know, she never missed a game."

I blink, not following him. "Huh?"

"Claire. She went to every single game you ever played." Mr. Woodley sticks another forkful of salad in his mouth and chews, like he hasn't just rocked my whole world.

Claire hates sports. She isn't the slightest bit interested in basketball. She was in college when I was in high school. He has to be mistaken.

I look at my fries and try to wrap my brain around my arguments. He is wrong. Dead wrong. "She was in college. She graduated from high school before I even started playing."

"She commuted. And yeah, we had some bad weather. She drove through it anyway. And I don't know whether she adjusted her schedule so she didn't have evening classes, or whether she skipped them. But she was there. For every game."

I watch barbeque sauce drip off the fries I'm still holding, not really seeing it and blinking as each thought zips through my head.

Did Claire graduate from high school and all of a sudden develop some kind of love for basketball? What was she doing going to every game?

"How do you know this?"

"Don't you remember what I used to tell you boys?"

"You told us a lot of things." I wasn't saying that sarcastically. It is true.

"I told you to practice trying to see everything. You needed to be able to sweep your eyes over the court and know what kind of defense the opposing team was playing, know where every player was, what direction they intended to go, and make split-second decisions based on everything you saw. You, especially, being point guard. You needed to know what play to set up, what defense you were going to run, and what kids to watch. You had to teach yourself to be observant and to not miss anything."

I nod. He had. He had often showed us pictures, given us three seconds to look at them, and then asked us questions about them. Improving our powers of observation.

It's what he claimed anyway.

"I practiced that myself," he says. "I would sweep my eyes over the stands. Then, later, I'd see if I could remember who was there. My wife helped me." He pauses here, and I know a little of the pinch of pain he must be feeling. Then he starts again. "It was something I'd gotten good at over the years. Just always learning, always trying to improve, always trying to be better. Because a coach needs to be able to do that too, you know. Have good powers of observation."

I nod. There are tons of times I could think of off the top of my head where he had seen things on the floor that I hadn't seen, but it stood to reason that he practiced and got better at catching the little details that really mattered in a game.

"I know."

"That's what I'm telling you. She was there every game. From the time you started in ninth grade, and you were good enough that you started, until your very last game, and every game in between—when you hit one thousand career points. When you hit two thousand career points. When you were named all-state. We went the whole way to Boise for the all-state game. She was there."

"She had a boyfriend then." I am sure of it. I think I might have mentioned the crush I had, although apparently it hadn't made me observant enough to realize she attended every single one of my games. I hadn't noticed at all.

"She might have. He never went to any games with her, though." Mr. Woodley shrugs, and it stands to reason he wouldn't have known if Claire had a boyfriend or not. His focus was basketball.

"She sat alone?"

"Sometimes, she sat with a sister. But yeah. She sat alone."

That changes things. When a person is in high school, or when a person graduates from high school and comes back for a game or whatever, they don't want to be alone.

For Claire to want to go to a game bad enough that she would go by herself and sit by herself…she was serious about wanting to be there.

"Why do you think she was at all those games?" I finally ask. I've already had a thought in my head about it, but it feels kind of wrong that she would have been at those games because the team was so good, especially when she didn't even like sports.

Mr. Harding had been about to put a bite of salad in his mouth, but he lowers his fork, and his eyes meet mine. His head tilts ever so slightly like he can't believe I don't know.

"You."

My stomach and heart bump into each other, and it takes a bit for them to get straightened out.

In the meantime, I have trouble breathing.

My mouth opens and closes. Several times.

"Me? You think she was at the games because of me?"

"I was coaching the games. I really wasn't staring at the stands, paying attention to what everyone was doing. But..." Here, his eyes twinkle. "You know my wife, she went to every game too. She called you guys her boys, since we never had children, and she loved you like her own. She's the one who pointed out that the only player Claire watched was you."

My mouth hangs open, like a broken screen door.

"After she said that to me, well, I was a coach, and I wanted to win, but yeah, I loved you boys like my own, just as much as she did. And I watched." His eyes, old and full of wisdom, meet mine. "She was right. Claire went to those games, every single one of them, because of you."

fifteen

. . .

Claire

ON FRIDAY, Mr. Haywood is my last client of the day. Of course, that is super nice since all I have to do to go home is walk next door. I even park my car in my driveway instead of his.

I have to admit I am a little nervous as I walk up the steps and onto the porch, knocking on the door.

I'm tempted to say I'm not sure why, but I know exactly why.

I've been thinking a lot about Trey.

He helped at the assisted living center without complaint. He was good with the girls, teasing them without being inappropriate, and was great with the residents there.

I didn't see him much, since he kind of disappeared in the sporting goods section of the supercenter while I spent all of my time in groceries and then at the cash registers.

I don't think any of the men that he was with actually bought anything, but as I checked out the last person and walked out of the store, they were all sitting there on the benches outside, laughing and telling stories.

Trey looked like he was having a good time. But I couldn't shake the feeling that he wasn't happy with me.

I know. In a world that is fair, he would be the head coach, and I would be the assistant. But no one wants to offend me by suggesting that, including Mrs. Pinkerton, the principal, or any of the school board members who are responsible for paying me. Because after all, I have lived in Good Grief all my life, and I'm obviously not going anywhere.

Trey on the other hand, left after graduating and really hasn't been back. He hasn't made any secret about the fact that as soon as his dad is straightened up, he is trucking back to Seattle.

Mr. Haywood opens the door, and I pull my head out of the clouds and greet him.

Trey has Mr. Haywood's nose and his chin too. And that twinkle in his eye.

"Come on in, girl. I think you're gonna be pleased with my progress." He holds the door for me as I walk in, and he closes it behind me.

He is doing a lot better. I'm mostly here to take a blood sample so we can adjust his blood thinner if necessary.

He developed a blood clot in his leg when he was in the hospital after his stroke, hence the follow-up care.

"I'm sure you have. I understand that there's a sweet lady in the picture that might be inspiring you to clean up your act a little."

I tease him some, because he's known me since I was little.

When the house beside the fire station came up for sale, my mom wanted to move to be closer to it, even though it was only a few doors down. That's how Cody and I ended up buying my childhood home. It was right about the time we got married, and I never actually moved out.

My parents did.

"How's your dad doing?" Mr. Haywood asks as he settles down in his chair.

I settle down beside him and get my iPad out. It is nice that almost everything has gone electronic, although paperwork is still a pain.

"He's fine," I say, looking down at my iPad and waiting for Mr. Haywood's information to come up.

"He hasn't retired from the vet clinic yet, has he?"

"I don't think he ever will. He loves it too much."

My dad's a veterinarian, and a good one. In a town like Good Grief, he does everything, but his specialty is small animals.

As you would imagine, he's quiet, an introvert mostly. My mom's the outgoing one. But growing up with him, we always had a menagerie of animals at our house. People would pick them up by the road, and since we don't have an animal shelter, they'd end up taking them to Dad, who has never been able to resist anything in fur, and he'd bring them home.

I guess I shouldn't say Good Grief didn't have an animal shelter. Our house was the animal shelter.

Mr. Haywood nods thoughtfully. "He was a smart man to get into something he loved. It's hard to be passionate about a dispatching job. I can't wait to retire."

I nod, knowing exactly what he's saying. Both of my parents love what they do. So do I.

Cody hated his job. That wasn't why we split, but I understand how miserable it could make a person when what pays the bills isn't something they enjoy.

I can see the bleakness on Mr. Haywood's face.

"I bet you miss all the guys that you talk to, though." From what I understand, there is quite a brotherhood amongst loggers. Even though they are very individualistic.

"I do. It's not a terrible job, but you can't get passionate about it."

"Maybe you'd like to try something else?" I tilt my head, looking at him. "Is there something you wanted to do and just never got to?"

"No. Not really." Mr. Haywood scrunches up his nose. I wonder if the "thing" he was passionate about was his wife. Maybe he lost his zest for living when he lost her.

He sighs. "I guess after raising Trey and seeing how good he was at basketball, I wish I had played when I was in high school. There's just such camaraderie among teammates, and they had so much fun working toward their goal. He spent so much time shooting hoops out in the driveway, until long after dark, then he was up in the morning before school, doing it again. He kept his grades up, too, because he knew he couldn't play if he didn't." Mr. Haywood clasps his hands together in front of him, a small smile on his face. "He learned so much about hard work and determination and grit and perseverance. Teamwork and getting along with people. He's still friends with a lot of the guys that he played with in high school. There's just nothing that bonds you together when you work hard for something and are as successful as what they were. I loved watching him and was always a little jealous because I never had that opportunity. I couldn't play sports. My parents needed me to work."

He isn't bitter, at least he doesn't sound that way, and I don't get the idea that it is a huge regret. Just one of those things that kinda nags at him.

The opportunity is long past.

I start asking him the questions I have on my form. My focus remains on my job and doing the best for him.

But I don't forget what he said.

That, combined with what Trey had been saying, doesn't exactly change my mind, but it makes me think that maybe there is more to basketball than what I've been thinking. Maybe there are positive benefits, things that the girls might be missing out on because I'm not doing it quite right.

Basically, I think that there isn't much to be proud of in a team that never wins a game. Not that winning is everything, but it is more fun —and takes more character to get there—than losing.

It will bond the girls together to strive for that win more than not caring. Which is what I've been teaching.

I finish up with Mr. Haywood, and I never do ask him the questions I wanted to about Trey.

———

I AM STILL THINKING about the things that Mr. Haywood said Saturday afternoon as I sit at the fire hall with the ladies' auxiliary. We've already cleaned the fire hall and taken stock of what is in the cupboards and what we need to purchase in order to do the last chicken dinner of the season.

Now we are all just sitting around chatting about who is getting married, who is having babies, and whether or not Good Grief is ever going to get that high-speed Internet line they promised during the last election cycle.

I'm just kinda sitting here, enjoying the fellowship of the ladies. Most of them are my mother's age and older. Their sons are the firefighters, and their daughters are in law work, and they run the auxiliary.

Until my mom became the chief, she was in the auxiliary, and she dragged us to every meeting, every dinner, every barbecue, and every fundraiser. We even washed the fire trucks. I spent countless hours polishing aluminum wheels.

The cool thing about it was I also got to ride in the parades occasionally. So, don't think that it was terrible. Because it wasn't.

Anyway, I guess it is a natural thing that I became a member myself.

Even though I don't really fit in with these ladies who are a generation older than me, I love listening to them and learning from them.

I've done the same thing with my kids too. Melody's here somewhere. Probably in a corner with her nose in a book, and Evie is here as well. There's a basketball hoop on the cement pad behind the fire hall, and she and a couple of the ladies' grandkids are out there shooting hoops.

Anyway, I'm just happy to be here and am not paying much attention until the conversation to my right catches my ear.

"She wanted to play this year, but she didn't want to be on a team that never wins a game."

I notice Mrs. German kind of looks at me out of the corner of her eye after she says that.

It's not said in a mean way. I don't take offense, even though I know immediately they're talking about the basketball team and about Mrs. German's granddaughter who played last year but didn't come back.

"Larissa told me the other day she was glad that she's in the Carroll school district. She didn't want to play on our team." Mrs. Boxer gives a self-conscious shrug when she meets my eyes. "It's nothing against you, Claire. They love you. Truly. But they want to win too."

Both old heads nod sagely, and I don't feel hurt, but I do feel guilty.

Mrs. German reaches out and puts a hand on my leg. She pats it, her fingers gnarled with big knuckles. The hands of a woman who's worked all her life. Kind and full of love.

I don't doubt that they want the best for me.

"Just remember, sweetheart, the Bible says *whatsoever thy hand findeth to do, do it with thy might.*" The wrinkles around her eyes deepen, and she looks at me over the top of her glasses. "That includes basketball."

Mrs. Boxer nods, and then they go on to say how happy they are that I am teaching the girls good things and encouraging them to help with the assisted living center, and weed the gardens of shut-ins, and make food for new mothers, and all the other things that we have done.

Truly, they went on and on. I know they are fine with me and with what I do with the team.

But I could still sense a little bit of disappointment. Because while they love those "good works," those ladies would also really like to go and see their grandchildren play ball games. It would get them out of the house and give them an excuse to socialize.

Except, their grandchildren didn't want to play basketball, because no one wants to be on a losing team no matter how many good works they are doing.

Mrs. Tucker, who has been quiet up to this point in the conversation, speaks softly. "My granddaughter said she wanted to join the team, and she didn't care how many games they lost." She gives a sly smile and looks at the other two ladies. "She said Mr. Haywood was dreamy."

I smile at the way Mrs. Tucker says it, but then—noticing the way that Mrs. German and Mrs. Boxer are looking at me—my smile freezes.

"What?" I ask, but I can see the wheels of their heads turning.

"That's one way to build your team. Get yourself a dreamy assistant coach."

I close my eyes and shake my head. Like I asked for an assistant.

This is not something I want to talk about. It's not something I want to think about. I already have trouble thinking about Trey way more than I should. I don't even want to go where those ladies are attempting to take me.

Plus, they've already given me enough things to think about.

I believe that. What they said. That everything I do I should put my heart and soul into. I've never believed any differently, even if I don't always try my hardest at everything.

It isn't an easy way to live, because, for instance, when you have your heart and soul invested in your marriage, and your husband comes home and announces that he's found someone else, it will devastate you. Just saying.

I can't help but feel like maybe I've done this with basketball, for similar reasons.

Of course, I'm not going to have my heart broken. But I know I'm not any good at basketball. And if I sink my heart and soul into trying, somehow, to be a good coach and actually win games, it's going to be devastating when we don't.

Not to mention, I really don't have a roadmap of how to get there.

But I believe I've started out in the right direction.

Tuesday, we're actually going to work on basketball at basketball practice.

It will be a small first step in the right direction.

sixteen

. . .

Trey

I WALK INTO "BASKETBALL PRACTICE"—USING the term very, *very* loosely—on Tuesday with mixed feelings.

My conversation with Mr. Woodley has changed the way I look at Claire.

Somewhat.

I have been seeing her as a good bit older than me and pretty much someone who would never look at me twice.

Mr. Woodley seemed to indicate that she had a huge crush on me when I was in high school.

There's such an age difference between us; she wasn't even in high school when I was.

That doesn't matter to me.

Not now.

It's the least of the things I care about.

Not that I'm thinking of a romantic relationship.

I'm really not.

But it makes me wonder, if she watched so many basketball games —Mr. Woodley had said every single one I ever played—how could she be so unconcerned about practices? And winning?

Still, the conversation I had with him really only served to make me more curious about her.

I'm kind of looking at her with new eyes as I walk toward the foul line where she always seems to start practice, chatting with the girls.

I realize there's one extra girl.

Do we have a new addition to the team?

She doesn't hear me until I'm almost on her, at least she doesn't turn, and she looks surprised when she sees me.

Maybe just my imagination, but her cheeks look red too.

Why?

"Mr. Haywood. I'd like to introduce you to the newest member of our team, Baney."

I glance at the girl and give her a smile. Not a very big one because I don't really like the way she's looking at me. Not in a terribly bad way, just more interested than she should be.

Then she shoots a sly look at Claire, glances at her teammates, and lifts her eyebrows.

I really don't like that.

It makes me feel like they're up to no good, but I can't imagine what in the world that could be.

I'll have to watch that they don't do anything to Claire, like put a snake in her locker or something.

"Okay, girls, like I said when you came, we're going to practice basketball today." Claire sounds very businesslike, but she does slant me a glance, like she wants to make sure that I'm noticing that she is keeping her word.

I've definitely noticed.

I'm thinking about all the things we could start with and forming an answer just in case she asks me what I suggest.

"Baney, you and Rachel will be on one team, with the other two girls on the other. Evie, you have to sit out until we need a substitute." Claire points at the ball Evie is holding. "You can throw the ball up so the girls can jump for it."

She looks back at the girls with her hands on her hips. "Now, remember, if you stop dribbling, you have to stop walking too. We got called for that a lot last year. Also, remember, you're not allowed to go outside that rectangular black line. I don't even think you're allowed to touch it with your foot. We got called for that some as well. You have to watch where you're standing. Okay, girls?"

She gives them a bright smile and starts walking toward the edge of the gym. "You guys can go ahead and start whenever you're ready."

She's made it the entire way to the sidelines, and I still haven't gotten my mouth closed.

I haven't gotten the expression on my face under control either.

Shocked outrage, maybe? Or just completely aghast with sincere disbelief.

She's just going to have them play?

With the admonishment to stop "walking" if they stop dribbling. And of course, to watch for the black line.

I'm typically not a swearing man, but strings of words that I would never say in front of these teenage girls run through my head.

I was really looking forward to this practice, and now, I'm really looking forward to it being over.

My head is hurting, and I want to close my eyes, except…call me an idiot, but I kinda like the way she looks when she's walking away.

She also seems pretty pleased with herself.

And she thinks she's pleased me. At least, that's what I read in the expression on her face.

Like she's come to a decision that I might have been right, and she is giving me everything I wanted.

How do I tell her this isn't even close?

I run a hand through my hair and turn away, just in case she looks back. I don't want to hurt her feelings.

My ex was always talking about her feelings and how I had no idea how to make her happy. Like it was my job to make her happy.

I don't think anybody could have made her happy, but she seemed to think I could and it was my responsibility to spend every waking hour trying.

That isn't nice. I guess I should say it didn't seem to matter what I did, nothing was ever right. She never thought I was putting enough effort into making her happy.

I even tried to use Mr. Woodley's teaching, the one where he'd taught us to notice things.

Didn't work. Not with the ex, anyway.

That is how I notice Claire's expression, though, and figure she probably thinks she is doing a really great thing for me.

Now what?

I shift, looking over, hooking a hand behind my neck.

She turns around, but thankfully, she looks at the girls first, and I am able to get my mouth closed.

I need to look down at my feet though, because I am still having a little bit of trouble with my expression.

I don't want to hurt her feelings, but I had been hoping for slightly more than "go play basketball, girls."

I walk over to the sideline and turn around, standing beside Claire, maybe slightly behind her, so she is sure that I am giving her deference as head coach.

She waits until Evie throws the ball in the air before she looks at me and speaks low. "You don't look like you're very happy. Are you having a bad day?"

The girls slap clumsily at the ball, and I turn my head. They giggle and chase after it, paying no attention to the out-of-bounds line.

Rachel grabs it, takes three steps, and then says, "Oh, that's right. I'm supposed to dribble." She gives a little shrug and then grins at the other girls. "Wait there, guys, and give me a couple of minutes. I haven't dribbled since last year."

I hear snorting, and I turn my head, seeing three boys, tall and athletic, standing in the doorway.

I guess they're probably on their way to the weight room, and they're probably part of the boys' team, which practices in the evening.

I can't blame them for snorting. But it was unkind, and I have a good mind to say something. Maybe they realize that as two sets of eyes track over to me, their brows raise, then they hit the third member of their group in the shoulder before they exit the doorway.

I put the boys out of my mind, feeling like we have bigger problems. If we want to win games. We're doing great if we don't care a flip about winning.

I care.

I will never convince myself that I don't care.

When Claire said we would actually practice basketball today, I got excited. When the team's at the bottom, the only way you go is up.

But I guess Claire and I aren't really seeing things eye to eye on this.

"There *is* something wrong, isn't there?" Now, her voice holds true concern. "Have you changed your mind about wanting to be the assistant coach?"

Her head turns back to the court, and she watches the girls as she speaks, like she doesn't care about my reaction or response.

That makes me feel like she really does care.

A lot.

And I think again about what Coach Woodley said.

And what Tammy said the day we chased Midget. I hadn't believed her then.

"So when I was in high school, did you have a crush on me?" I ask, knowing that question goes against all workplace harassment regulations and all accepted social norms as well.

I barely know her, and there I am, asking the thing on my mind rather than answering her question or contributing anything intelligent to the conversation.

"I did." Her mouth barely moves, and her words are hardly audible.

Her eyes stay on the girls, who are practically tripping over each other to be polite, to keep from getting in each other's way, and to give each other space.

I have never seen basketball played like this before.

Ever.

"What about now?" I ask.

I don't even know where that question comes from. But I realize immediately it's the thing I really want to know. The thing I never should have asked. But a man has to take a chance once in a while. Risk rejection. Nothing good comes by sitting around and waiting for someone else to bring it to you.

Basketball taught me that too.

It's a lesson these girls need to learn.

"I don't know." Claire turns her head and looks at me. I see on her face her answer is as honest as it can be.

"I had a huge crush on you up until the day you got married. It probably lasted a little longer, but I had hope up until that point. After that…" I shrug. "Because I just knew it was wrong." Her marriage didn't change my feelings, but it changed how I could act about them.

She nods and turns her head back to the girls. "That has something to do with basketball?" she asks, her voice a wisp in the air.

I stand there, my eyes on the girls, my heart thumping. I guess it does. I guess I feel like I have to lay it out for her before I can say what I want to.

"I'd like to actually teach these girls how to play basketball," I say.

This time, *my* eyes stay on the girls as I speak. I don't want to see her reaction. My whole body is tensed up, and I'm scared to death to hear what she's going to say.

I'm expecting an explosion. A rebuttal at the very least. Any kind of negative reaction. I don't expect it to go over well.

"I would too," she says, and I feel her eyes on the side of my face.

My jaw twitches, and I turn my head slowly, unable to hide my disbelief. "Really?"

She nods.

I don't know why, but my eyes drop to her lips. They're red and shaped like a bow, and they move in a tantalizing way as she quotes, "Whatsoever thy hand findeth to do, do it with thy might." Those lips close, and maybe a smile touches them before they open again. "If the girls are going to play basketball, I think they ought to do it to the best of their ability."

Her teeth come out, and they grab her bottom lip.

I have to look away. Not to her eyes. They're just as mesmerizing.

"But I don't know how… I…I hope you'll help me."

My breath pushes out, and while it's exactly what I want to hear, it's not *everything* I want to hear. It's not even what I want to hear most. But it's a start. It's a little more than a start.

I close my eyes and I take a breath, fortifying myself, before I open them again and turn to meet hers.

"I will."

After that, practice changes some. Not just for the day, but for the rest of October.

We switch practice to every day after school. I schedule three hours on Saturday morning, because the boys have the gym Saturday afternoon, along with voluntary attendance on Sunday after church. That comes with pizza. Provided by me.

Claire backs me on everything I say, and I clearly give her deference as the head coach.

I don't have any illusions about the team winning a championship. I do, however, have high hopes that they might win a game. Or two.

The good thing about the way Claire has been doing things is that the girls who are on the team are on the team because they really do want to play basketball.

It doesn't take too much to motivate them into jumping on the bandwagon, especially as I casually drop the fact that I was an all-state baller and part of the team that won the two pennants that are in the display case in the hall at the end of the gymnasium.

Hey, I believe in being humble, but I also believe in doing whatever it takes.

The whole time, it isn't just the girls learning to play basketball. It's also Claire and I learning to work together.

For me, that is the best part.

seventeen

. . .

Claire

FRIDAY NIGHT, my kids go to my mom's to stay overnight.

I've mentioned my dad is a vet, and the girls going over is mostly because of that.

It went down like this.

Through the years, when someone finds a stray animal, either along the road or hanging around their house or whatever, because there's no animal shelter in our county, they always take it to my dad. He has cages and everything at his clinic and can house the animals while he works to find the owners.

Of course, sometimes all the cages are full, and that's what happened on Friday night.

He has this cute little puppy, what we figure to be a miniature poodle mix, that had been brought in a couple weeks prior.

He has been working pretty hard to find its home because it seems like it is an expensive designer dog and someone paid a lot of money for it.

He's searched everywhere, and no one is turning up as an owner.

Then someone brought another dog in. This new dog is a pitbull, and while in my experience, pitbulls are actually very good with people and children and not so good with other animals, you just never know.

So, he took the puppy out to make room for the pitbull, and my mom, who knows if the puppy ends up at her house, they would most likely be keeping it, and they already have five dogs, offered to watch my kids if I kept the puppy.

That's how I came to be sitting in my living room Friday night, curled up with a blanket and book, Midget lying at my feet and staring with loving eyes at the puppy in my lap while I try to read.

My cats are offended, just because cats get offended over everything and not really because of the puppy, but they're hiding somewhere.

I am very sore.

Trey is working the girls hard at practice. At least in my eyes.

When I'm in charge, I've always been a big proponent of not asking people to do things that I wouldn't do myself, and so I've been trying to keep up.

Wednesday, he had them running what he called suicides.

It's Friday, and I am still hobbling around like an old woman.

If I weren't so stubborn, I probably would take a pain pill. Moving, any kind of movement, hurts.

I can't complain. Trey told me since I'm the coach, I'm not supposed to do the drills.

But...I guess coaching means something different to me. Because, like I said, I couldn't ask the girls to do things that I wouldn't do.

And I've never done suicides before.

Just to be clear, I am perfectly fine never doing suicides again.

The puppy shifts in my lap, and although I already have a dog big enough to be about six dogs, I am seriously thinking of keeping this one.

We have fostered enough dogs over the years that my girls were actually more excited to go to their grandmother's house than they were to play with the new puppy, so I am alone.

I've already cleaned up three puddles of puppy pee and two piles of the other stuff.

Otherwise, I'm enjoying the time by myself. My book isn't that great, and I am petting the puppy and thinking more than I am reading.

Okay. I am thinking about Trey.

I definitely have fun working with him. And yeah, I am thinking about how much I admire him and like him and how good he has been to me, and how he has given me deference, even though he is obviously the knowledgeable one about basketball.

But I am also thinking that maybe I should just give my position to him.

The nicer he is to me, the more I feel like he deserves it, since obviously he is the more qualified one out of the two of us.

Anyway, I waver back and forth with that and occasionally get distracted by thinking about what he'd said about his crush, although he's not done anything else like that in the week or so since. He's been nothing but completely professional.

Since Cody left, I haven't met anyone that I am interested in dating.

Not until Trey.

That isn't exactly the thing I want to think about, though, so having the doorbell ring is actually a welcome distraction.

I'm not expecting anyone and have no idea who it might be at this time of night.

But this is Good Grief, and I'm not apprehensive, just curious as I get up, setting my book down but holding the puppy, and walk to the door.

Midget beats me there.

Great Danes aren't exactly known for being wonderful watchdogs, and she slept right up until the doorbell rang.

I think she is less excited about announcing an intruder than she is about getting to see someone. Anyone.

And possibly getting to put her nose on the puppy again. It was love at first sight for Midget.

I grab Midget's collar to keep her from knocking down—in love of course—the person at the door.

That leaves me in a bit of a dilemma, since I have the puppy in the other hand and don't want to put it down. Since it has been an hour and a half since I last took it out, it is almost guaranteed to pee on my floor again.

After about three seconds of thought, I finally pull back on Midget's collar and shout at the door, "It's unlocked. Come in!"

There is a three- or five-second pause while the person on the other side of the door apparently waits and tries to decide whether I actually mean that or not.

I am trying to figure out if I could possibly tuck the puppy under my arm and grab the door that way when it creaks open.

My heart skips, then does some suicides of its own when Trey appears on the other side.

We said goodbye after basketball practice. I did my best to pretend my entire body was not aching, and I didn't expect to see him again until tomorrow's basketball practice.

In all the time that he's been living with his dad, the only time he's been at my house was the day Melody almost burned it down.

"Um…hi," I say awkwardly, struggling to keep a hold of Midget and the puppy.

"So the small pony wasn't enough? You got a new dog?"

Apparently, whatever he wants, it's not an emergency since we are going to do some small talk first, I guess.

"Not exactly. Dad just ran out of room at the clinic."

His head jerks up. I think he probably understands.

Everyone knows my dad's clinic doubles as the animal shelter. Living beside us over the years, he's seen some interesting animals coming through our house.

We had a monkey for two weeks, a couple of goats over the years, several potbellied pigs, and thankfully the three boa constrictors dad had kept at the clinic.

Mom had insisted.

Trey glances down at Midget. She is still straining to get to him.

"You can let her go. I'm not afraid of her."

I try not to sigh in relief. Normally, I don't allow Midget free rein if we have houseguests.

She can be overwhelmingly nice and accidentally hurtful. But it is a bit much since now the puppy is struggling to get out of my arms and go greet the newcomer as well.

"She'll only sniff you for a few minutes, and she doesn't usually jump up," I say as I let go.

He scratches Midget's head, which comes to his chest, and leans his head down so Midget's nose almost touches his.

That's just wonderful. On top of everything else, he has to be good with my dog too.

If the cats like him, I'm sunk.

I figure there's no need to worry. My cats don't like anyone.

Midget usually overwhelms people. They aren't used to a dog that big.

"For such a large dog, she's really sweet," he says.

"She is. A big baby. Couch potato, really. But watch her tail," I say as she turns. "It feels like a stick against your legs when she's this excited."

He jerks his head and doesn't flinch when her tail smacks against his knee before Midget moves off.

"You can come in," I say, assuming he isn't here for a visit, but he isn't saying what he wants, so I don't know what else to do, other than stand there holding the door and looking dumb.

"I am, uh, sorry to bother you."

I wave my hand, my fingers still burning from Midget's collar, and remind myself to move smoothly and not like the old lady I was allowing myself to be when no one could see me.

"It's not a bother. The girls are at my mom's, and I'm just enjoying a little bit of time to catch up on my reading."

I most certainly do not add that I've been thinking about him more than I've been thinking about my book.

"Well..." He shifts his feet and clenches and unclenches his hands. Weird. "This is maybe a little unusual, but I wondered if you might have some spinach I can borrow."

I'm sorry. I have to admit my head tilts way to the side, and I give him a look that probably is as confused as I feel.

"I actually do have some in the refrigerator," I say, although it's an automatic answer.

My mind is trying to figure out what in the world he could possibly want spinach for this time of night? It has to be almost eight o'clock.

I start walking toward the kitchen, and he follows me.

"I've been trying to get my dad to eat some healthier things, and I went to make him a spinach salad, and I realized that I neglected to pick up spinach at the store."

"It's okay. You could be using it to try to make a battery to run your phone, you don't have to explain. I'm happy to let you…not borrow… *have* it." I lift an eyebrow as I open the refrigerator door. The puppy has snuggled down in my arm.

"Yeah. When I said borrow, I meant that I'll grab some at the store and pay you back. I'm not used to the grocery stores closing so early. In Seattle, many of them are open until eleven if not all night."

I nod. "Small towns, right?"

"Actually, I've been enjoying the small town. Things that were annoying to me as a teenager are kind of nice now that I have some years under my belt." He puts a hand on his stomach. "I know what you're thinking. That's not all I have under my belt."

He gives his self-conscious grin, and I pause in the process of pulling the bag of spinach out of the refrigerator.

Seriously? Is he insecure? It strikes me as odd. Our town practically worships at his feet everywhere he goes, since he is the only all-state baller ever to come out of Good Grief.

"I wasn't thinking that," I say. Honestly.

I finish pulling the spinach out of the refrigerator and shut the door.

I turn to face him, handing the bag of spinach over. His expression is serious.

"I want to thank you too." He takes the bag, and it crinkles, loud in the silence of my kitchen.

"For the spinach? Of course. Anytime. That's what neighbors are for." I say this flippantly, because his serious tone and expression have made me uncomfortable. I don't like serious conversations. Especially ones that are emotionally charged as I suspect this one will be, although I can't put my finger on exactly what makes me feel that way.

I start to move, but his words stop me.

"For that, yes. But also for what you've done with the basketball team. And what you allowed me to do. It means a lot to me, and I think it's going to end up being a season that the girls will never forget."

There are so many things running through my head right now. Things I want to say.

It should be me thanking him. I've heard, although it hasn't happened yet, that another girl is going to join the team. Just because of Trey.

I've also heard there's a buzz in the school, a buzz of excitement because of the all-state baller being involved in the program.

I've also heard, and this could just be gossip, that the school board is thinking of springing for new uniforms for the girls as well.

This is huge, since the uniforms they're wearing are twenty years old.

All because of Trey.

"Are you really just hanging out here tonight by yourself?" he asks, and it sounds like there's hesitation in his tone.

"Yes." My word sounds defensive, because I feel like me hanging out at my house by myself on a Friday night, while it's exactly what I want to be doing, makes me a loser.

In the eyes of the rest of the world, I probably shouldn't be alone on Friday night and happy about it.

But I can't think of anything else to go with that word, and it gets quiet again.

eighteen

. . .

Trey

I CAN ALMOST FEEL the shock that goes through Claire as my question hangs in the air.

I don't even know why I bother.

She obviously wasn't expecting me tonight. Not that she should have been.

My ruse of borrowing spinach, of all things—what in the world made me think to say spinach?—I mean a cup of sugar, sure. Neighbors do that all the time. Or flour. Or even milk. But spinach?

That was real slick there, Trey.

It's obvious that she questions my sanity. But at least she hasn't questioned my story. If she had pressed, I would have had to admit that we've already had supper, the dishes are washed and put away, and nobody is eating anything else at our house until at least tomorrow morning. And we aren't having spinach salad for breakfast.

But thankfully, she didn't press. Although, I don't think she really believes me either.

Still, she lets me stay. And now I'm not sure what to do. I don't want to make things awkward at practice. But I also just want to have a conversation with her between two regular people and not between the head coach and her assistant.

And not with a bunch of girls giggling at us.

"Do you want to come in and sit down?"

"Thank you."

Racking my brain for something to talk about, I follow her into the room. I'm thinking so hard about what I'm going to say I barely notice that she's stopped.

Okay, correction there. I don't notice that she stopped, and I run into her back.

She stumbles forward, and I reached to catch her, but I miss.

She steadies herself at the table and turns slowly. My stomach cramps, because she seems like she's hurt.

"I'm so sorry. You're hurt."

She shakes her head. "No. I..." She looks down and seems a little sheepish. "I'm still sore from the suicides that you made the girls run on Wednesday."

"I told you not to do them." I can't keep myself from laughing.

"I know. That's why I've been trying to pretend I'm not sore. Once I start moving around a bit, it pretty much goes away."

"Yeah. Take a couple pain pills, and you'll be good for the day."

"I know. I should do that, I just..."

"You're too stubborn to take pain pills."

She nods. Her sheepish look intensifies. Man, it's a cute look on her.

"Oh. Hey. Before we sit back down, I probably ought to take the puppy outside. She's not really housetrained." She looks at the clock on the wall. "I guess it's time for Midget to have her evening walk too. Do you mind?"

"If I were less secure than what I am, I would think that you're thinking of excuses to not have me inside sitting with you. But since I have overpowering confidence, I'm going to assume that you really mean that."

"I do." She quirks her lips and looks at the spinach in my hand. "Do you want to take that to your house?" Her eyebrows go up, and her eyes narrow slightly.

It's my turn to look sheepish. "It can probably wait. I *am* making spinach salad, but I wasn't going to do it until tomorrow for lunch."

She smirks at me, and I know I'm smiling, but I'm also thinking about how we worked together all week at practice and how much I've enjoyed it. How she didn't let her ego and everything that she'd been planning get in the way of her listening to my ideas and being willing to change her mind.

"Would you like to hold the puppy?" she asks, grabbing Midget's leash from a hook next to the door.

It seems kind of silly for me to hold the puppy while she struggles with the dog/pony. I hold my hand out for the leash.

"If you don't mind, I'd like to get to know Midget a little better. I see you and your daughters walking her at night, and with her size and regal carriage, she's definitely an eye turner. Plus, she's so sweet."

I mean that. Midget truly is a lot bigger than I'm used to a dog being, but she has an amazingly kind and gentle personality to go along with her size.

"Look at her," Claire says.

My brows crinkle and I glance at Midget, who's looking at the puppy with absolute adoration in her big brown eyes.

"It looks like it's love. That's not a boy, is it?"

Thankfully, Claire laughs at that. It could've been an awkward question. Of course, I didn't realize it until it was out of my mouth.

"No. She's a little girl."

"I suppose you don't want to name her in case you're not keeping her?" I ask. It seems a little awkward to keep calling her The Puppy.

"That's right on. We had that happen so many times growing up, where Dad would bring some animal home, and we'd all fall in love with it, and we'd beg him to let us keep it, and he'd finally say yes, and then the owner would show up."

"That's tough."

I suppose on some level I know that was probably a good thing. Suffering usually is. It produces character growth, anyway.

Just like sports, where you run suicides—my mouth crinkles at the thought of how adorable Claire was as she insisted on running with the girls—it hurts, and it's painful, but it makes you better.

Still, it's never easy to lose something you love.

"It was. I think it was just as hard for my parents though. I mean come on, there were four of us girls, and I'm sure you can imagine, and maybe you even heard at times, the weeping and the wailing that occurred when that happened."

"Now that you mention it, I do remember a time or two walking out and hearing really odd noises coming from your house." I allow my eyes to lower and look at Claire's stomach. "But as I recall, it was close to suppertime, and I just assumed they were stomachs growling."

She laughs, and I realize I've come to love the sound. I want to hear it over and over.

I think of the puppy and falling in love and losing things and how I had just thought that was a character-growing experience.

But it's a good character-growing experience for someone else. Not for me.

I've gotten Midget's leash snapped onto her collar, and Claire moves to the door. "Are you ready?"

I put my hand on Midget's head, amazed at how silky she feels, and I say, "We are."

"You do need to keep a good hold on her, because she pulls almost all the time, but when she sees something she wants, it can be a real job to stop her."

"I think I'm up for the challenge."

I have total confidence in my ability to hold the dog. I figure she probably weighs about as much as I do. However, maybe I'm being arrogant, but I think I'm slightly smarter than she is.

And brains are better than brute strength.

Most of the time.

Still, because I don't want to embarrass myself in front of Claire, I slip my hand through the leash end, bracing it on my wrist and gripping the leash with my hand, figuring that it's probably better to be safe than sorry.

We step out, and Claire closes the door behind us. While I'm waiting for her, I say, "She'd probably like one of those retractable leashes. That might be easier."

"Probably. But it's so hard to find one that's heavy-duty enough to hold her. We tried a couple different ones, and they always end up snapping."

"I guess having a dog this size presents more than a few challenges."

Claire chuckles, and I like that sound too. It's not as good as a laugh, but it's close.

We start off by going out the back side of her lot and walking up the alley behind our houses. If we take a right down at the corner, the alley goes up, passes a couple more houses, and then winds through the woods until it comes out on the back road that goes down by the river.

I assume we're not walking that far and will turn around at some point. There aren't any houses, and with the almost full moon, it's a beautiful night for a walk.

"It does," Claire agrees. "One of those challenges is trying to find room on the couch to sit down. I suppose if we'd been smart, when she was a puppy, we would have taught her to stay off the couch. Now, and I'm not kidding about this, Melody, Evie, and I will sit on the floor, and Midget sits on the couch."

"That sounds like a spoiled dog."

I like it though. It shows so much of Claire's personality. She was willing to give up so much to make the basketball team better but also for me—her thoughts of what the basketball team should be, her ideas of what they'd do at practices, and her goals of using those things to build character and community spirit in the girls. She's deferred to me at practice when it comes to technique, drills, and plays, even though I don't have any right to have a say.

That she'd give up her couch for the dog makes me laugh, but it also makes me respect her in ways that just reinforce what I already know about her.

Midget jerks at the leash, and I remember just in time to keep a tight hold. My mind is wandering, and I wasn't exactly close to losing her, but I know I need to be careful and pay attention.

"She is strong."

"She is. But she's also so sweet. I mean, seriously, she sometimes doesn't realize how big she is, and she can just brush into little kids and knock them down. But she doesn't mean to hurt anyone, and she never does it on purpose."

"I know. You love your dog."

"Why don't you have a dog?" She asks the question easily. We're just having a light conversation. I don't want to get too deep. But I don't want to avoid the question or lie either.

"My wife was allergic to dogs. We had cats."

"Oh? I've never seen them at your dad's house."

"She got the cats and the kids in the divorce."

"You gave them up to keep from fighting?"

"The boys loved the cats. It'd be dumb of me to lose my kids yet fight for the cats."

"I see." She puts her head down and walks along, stopping with the puppy as it sniffs something along the edge of the road. After a few moments, it starts walking again.

"I'm impressed that Midget isn't stepping all over the puppy."

"No. She's really good about that. I was worried about that to begin with. But it turned out to be unfounded."

"Maybe you'll be able to keep her."

"Is it terrible that I want to?"

"A little. After all, Midget's enough dog for about four families."

We laugh together, and I'm loving it. The dark, the moon, the easy laughter.

I want more.

But I figure I'm not there yet.

She deserves to know where I want to go.

I debate with myself for about two seconds before I open my mouth. "I don't want to make things awkward for basketball practice, but I really like being with you. If you remember, I mentioned that I really...liked you before we were both married, and I've found, with being around you again, those feelings aren't buried too deep."

Our feet crunch as the blacktop ends and we begin to walk on stones.

There are two tire tracks, and it would make more sense for me to walk in one and let her walk in the other, but I walk in the middle.

Because I want to be close to her.

I think I'm falling.

It takes her a while to answer, but I don't worry about it, because I think she likes me too. After all, we're walking together. And laughing together. And talking easily.

"I think it might be better for us to stay friends only. At least until basketball season is over."

I am not expecting her to say that. It makes sense, and I'd actually thought the same thing myself. But I kinda thought we could take a few steps forward, and it would be okay. I thought she'd want to.

It's my turn to walk quietly. And I kick myself while I'm doing it.

There goes the lighthearted mood. I've ruined everything.

There's a long silence, and I feel like an idiot.

It surprises me when she speaks. "Are you staying in Good Grief?"

My mind screeches to a stop. I consider her question.

I'm not considering the answer to it exactly. I know the answer. Although, it doesn't crystallize in my mind like I expect it to. The word "no" doesn't trip off my lips like it should.

Maybe that's why she stiff-armed me. Maybe it has nothing to do with us coaching basketball together and everything to do with her being worried that I am just here until my dad gets better and then leaving again. Which, to be fair, was my plan.

But when I was asking her about being more, I wasn't thinking that she and I would go to Seattle together.

I am thinking, to be honest, about…staying…staying here. Here in Good Grief, Idaho.

Those words, that thought, the concreteness of it hadn't formed in my head until just now. Maybe I'd had an inkling, but I hadn't really articulated it, not even to myself.

"That's what I thought," she says before I can say anything. I mean I had plenty of time to talk, I just haven't figured out what I am gonna say.

"No. Wait. I…I was thinking. I didn't want to say something that wasn't true." I say this honestly. And to Claire's credit, she seems to believe me.

I love that. It makes the words come easier to my mouth as my thoughts crystallize.

"When I moved here, my sole thought was to help my dad and go back to Seattle. But when I said about us just now, I wasn't thinking about us as a fling."

"You are thinking about us as in you in Seattle and me in Good Grief?"

"No. I hadn't really thought about it exactly, but that's not what I want."

"I'm confused."

"I'm not. Not really. If there were a reason for me to stay in Good Grief, that's what I want to do."

There. I am being as honest and open as I can be.

She's already rebuffed me once, and I don't want to have to go through another rejection. Not two in the same walk anyway.

The puppy starts lagging behind, and Claire bends down, scooping her up and holding her tucked against the opposite side from me.

Midget isn't nearly done with her walk, and we continue on in silence.

Maybe I should move over to my tire track, but I stay in the middle with Claire walking right beside me.

She didn't tell me a direct no. Just "wait." I can do that.

She's worth the wait, however long it is.

She's worth the hope that there will be more.

There's a little bit of a hump in the middle of the road, and when Midget jerks on the leash, I lose my balance slightly.

Not a big deal, but the backs of our hands brush.

I feel a little like I'm in high school again as I try to think of a way to lose my balance and fall into her again.

But I'm too old for tricks like that, and I shove those thoughts aside.

No sooner have they gone out of my brain than our hands brush again.

This time, I haven't lost my balance. Midget hasn't pulled me at all. And there is no reason for Claire to waver, since she is walking in the tire track.

Regardless, it makes me smile. I'm still enjoying the thought that she might have touched me on purpose when our hands brush again.

This time, I'm sure she did it on purpose.

Maybe she can see my teeth in the moonlight as I look down at her.

She has an innocent look on her face, and when she feels my eyes on her, she looks off to the side, the corners of her lips dipping up just slightly.

I look straight ahead again.

I'm waiting for it when, not twenty seconds later, our knuckles brush again.

It does surprise me, however, when this time, instead of a light brush, her fingers slide into mine.

It's funny, how I feel that touch, this movement of her skin, the twisting of my stomach, and the lifting of my heart all at once.

I love that I feel her touch the whole way through my body.

I stare straight ahead, and I take three steps before I say, with a smile in my voice, "I thought we were going to stay just friends."

"Don't friends hold hands?" Claire asks, total innocence in her voice.

"I don't think so."

"Can we be friends at basketball practice and maybe the holding hands kind of friends at night when we walk the dogs?"

"I think you just asked me out on a date."

"I asked you out on a lot of dates. I walk the dogs every night."

"You…usually have your girls with you." I need to know where she's planning on going with this. I'm content to let her lead. I feel like she likes me, and I know I like her, and I can respect it if she's not quite ready to say any more. I can respect that and trust that we'll keep spending time together, and if she hasn't already fallen in love with me, maybe she will.

"I know."

"And you're okay with being holding hands friends while we walk the dogs with your girls?" I ask, because I want to be clear.

"Yes." Her word's firm, and I think my heart is doing a victory dance. Either that or it's taken up kickboxing.

My thumb brushes over her hand, and I say, "Are you sure?"

"Yes."

I love the confidence in her voice and the way she doesn't hesitate. I feel like things have almost come full circle, in a way, since I'd had such a big crush on her. Then, after she got married, and I went away to college, I never thought that there would be anything between Claire and me.

I can't say thoughts of her didn't go through my head at times as I lived my life, but I'd given up on my high school dreams. I'd moved on. Or so I thought.

I suppose my head is in the clouds, and when her thumb brushes mine, it makes all kinds of crazy things happen to all the organs in my body.

That's the only excuse I have because right as she brushes her thumb back over my knuckles, Midget sees a squirrel or something, and she takes off toward Claire's side of the road.

I jerk toward Claire, and maybe I would have been able to stop Midget, but I'm more concerned about keeping Claire from falling, and my focus is there rather than the leash that is slipping off my wrist.

When I'm conscious that it's almost slipped off, it's too late.

"I'm sorry. Are you okay?" I ask, a little breathless, because I'm surprised and flustered, and despite the fact that I know I need to go after her dog, I've got my arm around her waist, and I really don't want to let go.

Maybe there's not that much difference between high school me and the middle-aged adult me.

"I'm fine." She leans away from me, and I think she wants to put distance between us, but then she was just moving away so she doesn't shout in my ears as she calls, "Midget! Midget! Get back here."

I drop my hand anyway, because having it around her wasn't part of our deal, even though I don't want to.

It's funny, because I'm not a walk through the woods kind of person, but I don't hesitate. "I'll find her." I step into the woods, brushing by leaves and branches and pushing others out of the way.

I can hear Midget crashing around not that far away, and I think I'll be able to get her.

"Midget. Come here, girl." Maybe we bonded enough that she'll actually come.

It's a lot darker here in the woods than it was out on the road, with the trees and leaves blocking the moonlight.

I'm holding my hands out in front of me so I don't walk into anything jagged, and vines scratch my arms, but I feel like Midget is not that far away.

I kind of wish I'd worn pants, rather than the shorts I threw on, as something scratches my shin, but I push the thought away, because I see a shadow moving and I'm pretty sure that's Midget right ahead.

Belatedly, I remember my phone in my pocket. I can use a flashlight app.

I grab my phone, pulling up the app and flicking the light on.

I don't know if that's what drew Midget, or if it was me calling her, but barely ten seconds after I turn the light on, she comes bounding to my side.

She licks my face as I push a vine out of the way and lean down, grabbing the leash. I put my hand through the loop, determined she will not get away again.

"Trey? Trey, did you get her?" Claire's voice comes through the woods.

I hear a stick snap, and I speak quickly, not wanting Claire to come through the briars.

"I've got her. Just stay there. You don't need to come in here, there are briars and stuff."

"Thank you." There is a ton of relief in her voice, and I grin to myself. I think I just scored some brownie points.

I tug on Midget's leash. "Thanks, girl."

As I start to walk, my light falls on leaves, bright red and clustered in groups of five. I'd just been standing in them, brushing them away from my face as I petted Midget and got the leash.

I blink and look a little closer.

Is that poison oak?

nineteen

. . .

Claire

SATURDAY MORNING, I wake up smiling.

It's a fantastic day. The sun is shining, and I had a wonderful time with Trey last night.

After Midget ran away, we kinda hurried back home and he left right away, even forgetting his spinach, which I actually ran over to his house.

I know I didn't have to, but I just wanted to see him again.

I think chasing Midget through the woods kind of ruined his good mood because he was a little withdrawn after that, but he'd told me he liked me, and he knew I liked him, and I might be past forty, but I felt like a teenager again. Honestly.

There are a few differences, of course. One major one being that we both have kids of our own.

But that exciting feeling of not being able to stop thinking about someone, feeling like you can't wait to see them again, wondering what he is doing and how soon I would talk to him is coursing through my body.

Honestly, I can't wait to get out of bed and see him at practice.

Melody and I are cooking breakfast, and I'm humming under my breath.

Melody doesn't notice because she's thinking about carbon and atoms in the experiment that she's been working on now for two weeks or more.

I know she's in her head, so I don't try to talk to her as we work side by side, me making toast and buttering it and her cooking eggs with me occasionally giving her direction.

Evie has taken the dogs out for a walk, which usually takes at least twenty minutes, so I'm surprised to see her bursting in the door not five minutes after she left.

She's excited, which of course means Midget's excited, which of course means there's a lot of thumping and bumping going on as her tail bangs into the refrigerator and the cupboard doors and slaps my thigh.

"Mom! Mom! You won't believe what happened to Mr. Haywood."

I feel like there's a ton of chaos in my kitchen, even though it's just a dog and my daughter. She's holding the puppy whose little face looks adorably curious and sweet.

I want to keep her.

"What?" And then I realize what she said. She's talking about Trey.

My heart flips, and my knuckles whiten as I clutch the butter knife in the air and take two steps toward my daughter.

"What? What happened?"

"He said he was going to text you. But he's going to the emergency room. He wants you to cancel practice this morning, because he's not going to be able to make it—"

"Wait," I interrupt her. "The emergency room? Is it his father?"

I take another two steps toward the door, but I don't know what I think I'm going to do. I'm a nurse, yes, but if his dad needs the emergency room, I'd just slow him down.

"No. It's him."

I gasp. "What happened?"

Visions of him bleeding to death, with broken limbs, or passing out on the way to the hospital fly though my head. My heart pounds like I've run a mile.

I take three more strides toward the door. "He shouldn't be driving himself to the hospital."

"Mom. He's already gone," Evie says, her brows furrowed.

Her words stop me, for now. But I have a good mind to drive to the hospital just in case I'll see his disabled car along the road somewhere with him lying dead inside of it.

I'm starting to get worked up again and start looking for my keys.

Evie's voice stops me again. "He just had a rash. It was all over his face and arms. It was red, and he had little white bubbles in it. He said it was really itchy too."

I stop short, and just as the words "poison oak" go through my head and I think about his walk through the woods last night in the dark, my phone dings on the counter.

Our kitchen isn't that big, but I jog back over to the counter and grab my phone.

> Would you mind canceling basketball practice this morning? Please. I seem to have developed a severe case of poison oak. I'm going to the ER, and hopefully, they'll take care of it. Would you keep an eye on my dad too, please?

He's texting and driving. Unless he stopped at the one stop sign at the intersection south of town.

I type out a quick text.

> I'll take care of basketball and your dad. I'm sorry about the poison oak. Thanks for last night.

I hit send before I can change my mind about that last sentence.

He already knows I had a really great time, but I can't help telling him again.

I suppose the man is getting the idea that being with me could be dangerous to his health. I have caused quite a bit of disruption in his life.

I determine that I will try as hard as I can to not cause him any more problems.

———

THE MONTH HAS FLOWN BY, and it's time for our first game.

Thankfully, Trey recovered from his bout with the poison oak no worse for the wear.

Not much worse for the wear. His trip to the ER didn't exactly take all the rash and itch away, but they were able to clean his skin and get most of the oil off so that the rash didn't get worse.

Anyway, it cleared up without any complications, and Trey didn't miss a night of going with the girls and me on our evening walks with our dogs.

The girls talked me into a front carrier for our little stray, who we have named Jello. No one ever came to claim her, even though we advertised and dad had a sign up in the vet clinic. So, without really making a conscious decision on it, we've kept her.

I try not to worry about her since my sister, Leah, is watching her. Normally I take her everywhere. I even carry her during practices. I actually take her to work with me too. Not into clients' houses—she stays in a small carrier in the car while I'm working with clients—but she goes everywhere with me.

She's kind of emotionally needy.

I can relate to that. Even though I know she doesn't have an ex that convinced her she was worthless, I can still relate.

I'm thinking about her now as I walk out of the locker rooms behind the girls, Trey beside me.

It's kind of funny the coaching routine we've fallen into.

I am the encourager and the one who's always looking for lessons. And of course, I deal with all the emotional issues the girls invariably have.

Trey deals with technique and drills and basically everything that relates to actually playing basketball. Or about building a foundation for playing basketball.

Even though I still retain the title of head coach, and he's still officially my assistant, we're definitely more like co-coaches.

I feel like it's worked out really well. And despite myself, I'm excited about our first game.

It's unbelievable how much the girls have improved. Even I can see it.

I did watch more than a few games of basketball when I was younger.

Maybe I should say I watched Trey play more than a few games of basketball when I was younger.

Still, a person can't watch as much basketball as I did while I was watching him without learning a thing or two.

I think our girls are going to win tonight.

I think Trey isn't quite as optimistic, but I know he's hopeful.

Maybe, I just want the girls to win for Trey.

And for them.

Because they've worked hard.

Trey's really great at laying out what they need to do, and if I can ring my own bell, I'm pretty good at motivating them.

Pizza helps.

Trey has Evie starting as point guard, and of course, Rachel is our center. We actually had another girl join the team, so we have six players—a little depth to our bench. Maybe not depth, but hey, we have a bench.

I'm not going to give you a blow-by-blow of the game.

Just know that there are two seconds left on the clock, and we are only down by one point.

I feel like that in itself is a small miracle.

Kenzie is standing at the foul line, and she has two shots coming.

The gym is absolutely quiet.

Normally, the opposing team's fans make a lot of noise to distract whoever is shooting, but there aren't too many people from the opposing team who showed up. I'm pretty sure they figured there wasn't going to be much of a contest. I think the few who are here are too stunned that we might actually beat them that they've forgotten they're supposed to be good fans and distract our shooter with a bunch of crazy noise.

They're from an hour and a half away, and though gossip travels like wildfire in a small town, the fact that Trey is helping me coach hasn't quite jumped over the mountain to that small town yet.

Unfortunately, Kenzie misses both shots.

And we lose by one point.

I don't think the girls care.

There is a huge celebration on the sidelines after we slap hands with the opposing team.

That's the closest game we've had in three years.

So yeah, now our record is oh and thirty-seven but to lose by only one point?

Everyone goes home happy. Including me. I'm pretty sure we're going to win at least one game this year.

I'm excited. More excited about that than I ever thought I would be.

And, yeah, maybe I'm excited about Trey, too.

He looked good when he played ball back in high school.

He looks even better as a coach.

twenty

. . .

Trey

I HAVE TO ADMIT, I'm excited about the girls' basketball team. Evie, despite her young age, is as good as any of the girls we play against, and she will most definitely be the next Allstate baller to come out of Good Grief.

Not this year. She's too young. But I'm proud of her, and proud of what the girls have accomplished.

Going into the third game, I don't really have any expectations that we'll win, but I do have expectations that we will play a good game.

I do, just to be clear, know that we will win a game this year.

I'm not entirely sure we're ready to win this one.

The other school is bigger than we are, and, from the little bit that I was able to scout out about them, they don't have a terrible team.

But, then again, neither do we.

Now, just so you don't think I'm an awful coach, I do have confidence in my team. I have confidence in the skills we're building. I am just not entirely sure that we've been working on them long enough.

However, I'm looking forward to our first win. And not just because I want it, or because the girls deserve it.

I want to impress Claire.

I want that more than anything.

I suppose it's man-think to assume that if I win a basketball game with a team that has had no wins in the last thirty-eight games, she'll be impressed.

Maybe, if she hadn't been the coach of the team for those thirty-eight games.

Even though I kind of know there's a flaw in my logic, I still can't stop myself from wanting to do something that will make her see how wonderful I am.

Maybe, somewhere in the back of my head, I'm thinking she'll fall in love with me if she admires me enough.

Because I'm pretty sure I've already fallen in love with her.

How could I not? The spark was already there, from our childhood.

All I had to do was see her again, see that the woman she's become is even better than the girl she was, and I'm lost.

We play another tough game, a lot of man-on-man defense, and my team is getting tired.

This is exactly why I had them run all those suicides. Exactly why I push them during practice and try to build up their endurance.

For games like this.

The other team is getting tired as well.

I'm sure that coach has a similar program. Maybe it's just my imagination, but I think my girls have more left.

Maybe I'm just sure they have more heart.

Maybe they've figured out how badly I want to win, or that it would make Claire happy, and they push for her. I don't know.

Whatever it is, when the final buzzer sounds, the score is tied.

We go into sudden death overtime.

I love it.

I love the challenge and the excitement and the feeling that we've prepared for this, and worked for it, and all our efforts are paying off.

Maybe I convey that to the girls, I don't know.

I do know I'm pretty fired up, and I think they feel it too.

After we break our huddle and our five best players go out on the floor, I meet Claire's eyes.

Maybe my excitement is contagious to her as well, or maybe she's just feeling it anyway. But I can tell she wants to win just as much as me.

I grin at her, a confident, cocky grin, and I don't even try to make it anything else.

"We've got this one."

She smiles little. It looks a bit like a smirk, but even though her eyes crinkle, one brow lifts, as though she's saying *I'll believe it when I see it*. But in a good way, because I feel like she actually thinks she might see it.

Maybe it's the confidence, maybe it's our hard work, or maybe it is just our time, but we lose the jump, deliberately, and Evie grabs the ball from the other team's side of the court, dribbles to the three-point line and swishes it.

Exactly what we planned. The other team probably assumed that if we were going to get the ball, we'd go in for the automatic layup, the guaranteed points and best chance of a foul.

But I knew Evie could do it. I knew she'd make the shot. Especially because the other teams' defenders would be running to the basket.

She made that shot unopposed.

I am proud of my team.

We slap the other teams' hands, and I give my girls a pep talk in the huddle before I send them to the locker rooms to get showered and changed.

Some parents come over to congratulate me, and my eyes follow Claire as she follows the girls into the locker room.

I want to talk to her.

There aren't many people at the game, and the gym empties out quickly. I go to the coach's room, which is separate from the where the girls are showering and changing and wait for them to join me there. I'm eager to talk about what we did right, and eager to emphasize the reason that we do the basic fundamentals, including conditioning.

It is all for tonight.

Winning feels good.

I want to share the win with Claire.

I'm thinking about that, when Kenzie, her blonde ponytail flying behind her, charges into the coaching room.

"Mr. Haywood. Come quick! It's our dog!"

"I can't go through the locker room," I say, automatically, even as I stand up from my chair and start toward her.

"None of the girls are in there; they're all outside. We've lost Jello!"

I don't want to be seen coming out of the girls' locker room, but I run after her anyway, because she's already disappeared.

Thankfully, we're around the back of the school, in the corner that no one typically goes to, since that's where the school's small, self-contained septic system is.

There is a tiny, square brick building just off to the side of the school that houses the septic control panel, and some maintenance items. I was in it once, just out of curiosity, back when I was a kid.

Back then, there was a chair and a desk and an old computer monitor sitting on the counter, along with a few buttons and knobs on one wall. That was pretty much it.

I wasn't in there to be a troublemaker. So even though the lock for this building is on the outside of the door for some odd reason, probably having something to do with safety and the septic system, although I have no idea what, I never go in again. That day, I just ducked back out and went on my way. Curiosity satisfied.

But now, for some reason, the door to the septic control building is open a crack, and as I walk out of the locker rooms, Claire is standing in the middle of the group of girls, and they're searching all around, when one of the girls shouts, "There!"

She points to the septic control room. "I just saw Jello squeeze through that crack."

I noticed Leah, Claire's sister, is standing off to the side. I know Claire had said that she was getting Leah to watch Jello, so it doesn't surprise me to see her. What does kinda surprise me is that Leah doesn't seem too worried.

That strikes me as odd, but I don't stand around thinking about it. I hurry to the group of girls.

Claire has already left them, and has her hand on the septic control door, pushing it open.

"You'd better go help her," Evie says, looking at me with sincere concern in her eyes. "You know how she is about mice." Her tone drops a little at that, like she is confiding in me, and trusting me to keep her mother safe.

I admit, that makes me feel pretty good. That not only is she sending me after her mother, but she trusts me.

I didn't know if I'll ever be able to convince Claire to take a chance on me, or if she'll always see me as someone younger who happens to be a good ballplayer, but it is worth sticking around Good Grief for.

I really like that her daughter seems to look at me with something like, if not admiration, respect. And trust.

I'm not going to take that lightly.

"You're right. I'll go with her." I start after Claire, and she barely glances at me, as I come up behind her. She steps into the building.

It's dark in here. Back in high school I had never looked for lights or a light switch.

It has electricity, so I assume there are lights somewhere.

There is nothing on the wall right beside the door as I walk in though, so I step in further, digging in my pocket for my phone, so I can shine the light around on the walls.

"They said Jello came in but I don't see her." Claire's bending over, looking underneath the counter. There's no mistaking the concern in her voice.

I have my mouth open to answer when the door slams closed. I take a step back and have my hand on the knob when the lock clicks.

I know this should probably make me angry, but as soon as I hear the lock click, I put my head down and laughed softly to myself.

The girls are celebrating.

And, after losing thirty-eight games straight, I can't blame them.

I want to celebrate too.

"Can't you open it?" Claire asks, and I don't miss the thread of panic in her voice.

"I think Jello is fine," I say.

"What?" Claire asks, unable to see the connection between the door shutting and Jello's safety.

I explain. "I'm pretty sure the girls were just using that as an excuse to get both of us out here, so they could lock us in together. I think this is a celebration for winning the basketball game. If you text your sister Leah, I think you'll find out Jello is safe."

In the darkness, I can't see Claire's face but I can tell she's not moving, probably just standing there staring at me, processing my words.

It doesn't take long, and she whips her phone out of her pocket, the screen lights up and her thumbs fly over it.

She's barely sent the text, when I hear a buzz, and a new message comes in.

Her phone clicks off and her hand drops.

"You're right. Jello's fine. The girls thought this would be a fun and harmless way to celebrate. Leah said not to worry. She'll come back in an hour and let us out. Sorry."

"Hey. You don't have to apologize to me. This actually works out well."

"How do you mean?" she asks, a little suspicion in her tone.

This is my chance. Maybe it's the adrenaline still pumping through my body or maybe I just can't let this opportunity go, because I don't even think twice. "I've been trying to figure out how I can get you alone. I never thought of this, exactly, but it's a great idea. I couldn't have paid to have this happen any better."

"You're scaring me," she says, although there's humor in her tone. "Why would you want me alone in the dark by myself locked in a room I can't get out of? Tell me that you didn't do anything in Seattle that would have put you in prison?"

I think she's kidding about the prison thing. I think. I almost play along, walking toward her and grabbing her shoulders and growling, but I'm not entirely sure she's joking, and if she's not, then she didn't understand what I just said.

"I wanted to get you alone, so I can kiss you. That's it. Pretty sure that won't send me to jail, although I almost feel like it might be worth it."

Her breath sucks in, and I allow myself to smile because she can't see me. I love that I've surprised her. I hope it's a good surprise.

I figure I'll know here in just a couple of seconds.

I don't hear her step forward, but suddenly her body is touching mine, and I know…it was a good surprise.

Her hands go around my neck, and she presses against me.

I know I asked for this, but I wonder if I'm ready.

My hands, without me thinking about it, come up and touch her shoulders, run down her ribs and rest in the indent of her waist.

I don't mean to say I'm not ready, maybe I'm just not sure if our relationship is ready. I don't even know if she likes me.

Maybe she's excited by the idea of making out in the septic control room.

While I doubt that, I think I've admitted that I'm not exactly the best in knowing how women think.

I know guys who joked about making out here, back in high school.

"Claire?" I ask.

I'm not even sure what I'm asking. Maybe permission, but my head is already lowering, and one of my hands travel back up her back and I bury my fingers in her hair.

"What are you waiting for?" she whispers softly.

I smile. I don't know why she's doing this, but it's exactly what I want, what I've wanted for a while, and I feel I'd be a little crazy and a lot stupid if I don't take advantage of the opportunity.

So I do. Wanting it to be more than just a long-held dream, wanting it to mean something.

Maybe that's why I put so much into it. I don't know.

I haven't been able to tell her how I feel, not using my mouth and words, so, I do it with my mouth, without words.

I tell her that I'm falling for her with a gentle touch and a slight brush of my lips against hers.

I press a little more firmly and maybe she understands I'm saying I hope she feels the same.

Her lips open under mine. My fingers curl in her hair.

I accept her invitation, hoping she knows I'm telling her I want to be more. I want what's between us to be everything. That I'm not kissing her just because the opportunity is here, but I'm kissing her because I want to share everything I have with her. I want the same from her. I can't and won't accept anything less between us.

My heart is trying to climb into her chest, and she's pressed so tightly against me, I think it might be successful.

I've never kissed a woman like this before, and, I have to admit, I've never felt like this before, either. Dizzy, lightheaded, and never wanting to stop.

I suspect Claire might be having the same trouble.

Man I hope so.

My knees are weak, and I've never done this before either - I lose my balance.

We end up moving together, and somehow, our mouths stay joined while our bodies stumble to the side. My shoulder hits what I think is the control panel, and I don't know if I press some buttons or move some switches or what, but a sudden rumbling breaks the silence of the air, and it also finally breaks us apart.

I barely notice the rumbling, and honestly, my lips are searching for hers again, when she says, "What's that?"

"I don't care," I say. It's the honest truth. Finding her lips as the last sound leaves my mouth, I think maybe she smiles, but she's kissing me back, and I don't care.

Her hands demand I move closer, and her body is pressed against mine, but she lifts her lips a little, and says, sounding out of breath, "Do you think something's going to explode?"

My lips are already moving toward hers again, and I say the only three words I seem to be capable of. "I don't care."

I have the woman I want. I'm holding her in my arms. Her lips are soft and so sweet under mine, and I truly don't care at all what the rest of the world is doing.

twenty-one

. . .

Claire

SO, I never made the front page of the paper before.

Thankfully our hometown paper went out of business years ago, pushed out by the internet, and I'm not on the front page now.

I have to wonder though, if the paper were still in business, if I would be.

My mom's always been quite a character, but I think it would have embarrassed my dad if my mug shot had landed on the front page.

Okay, I don't exactly have a mug shot. But the school district isn't exactly happy to find Trey and I in the septic control room.

They probably wouldn't have found us if we hadn't bumped the control panel and drained what they called the "undigested water" out into the football field.

Apparently, whatever we bumped, set off an alarm someplace we couldn't hear. There is some kind of safety mechanism inserted in the system, for perhaps if someone had fallen in to the uncovered agitator tank, or something, I don't know.

Anyway, it is a pretty big thing, with state officials, federal officials, DEP, DER, and several other local, state and federal agencies involved.

In the end, a lot of people are upset, but it doesn't really harm anything, and Trey holds my hand throughout, which shouldn't make a difference.

But it does.

He also manages to whisper in my ear that if I hadn't been such a good kisser, none of this catastrophe would have happened.

Which of course, I respond to in the most mature manner I can and stick my tongue out at him.

I'm not sure why seeing that made him bend his head and kiss me again, but it does.

Not that I mind.

When he kisses the corner of my lips and calls me his cute catastrophe, I have to say… I have nothing but fond feelings for the septic control room.

Trey says he has nothing but fond feelings for his cute catastrophe.

I've no idea how anyone could consider me cute. I'm over forty, after all.

It seems to be obvious to everyone, because I hear it all the time, that the man adores me, so, I feel like I have no choice but to believe him.

He says he wants to marry me this summer and will take the girls and go camping for our honeymoon.

For a guy from Seattle, he's certainly gotten back to his small-town, Idaho roots.

I'm small-town, and I love it here. But I'm not sure I'm a camping kind of girl.

Still, if that's what I have to do in order to marry him, I'm in.

epilogue

. . .

Tammy

I AM PRETTY happy to do my part in getting Claire and Trey together. In case you haven't figured it out, I had Jello the whole time they were looking for her.

I won't admit this to just anyone, but I am also the one who suggested locking them in the septic control room.

I work at the school every day, and just being honest here, I do have kind of a secret fantasy about getting locked in with some honorable man, who adores me, and spending a pleasant afternoon with him there.

So, Trey is an honorable man, and he definitely adores Claire, and although it isn't exactly afternoon, I figure I can give her my fantasy.

Since it seems like I'll never be living it.

My ex said I was too straightlaced and serious.

I don't understand why that came as a shock to him. We dated for two years before we got married.

I didn't have a personality change in that time.

But, it's what he claimed, and I didn't argue with him.

I did fight him when he hired a big city lawyer and fought for custody of our two boys.

I lost.

I had not been prepared for any of it, and, maybe I became even more serious and straightlaced, kind of as protection.

If that's the way I was, I'm not going to risk having anyone else even look at me without knowing exactly what I am.

That way, there can be absolutely no miscommunication. No changing his mind after we have two children together and deciding I'm not what you want, and never was.

Maybe if I could be cute like Claire, but no, I'm straight, and serious, extremely tall and completely uninteresting.

Not cute.

Which is fine, I don't mind being alone.

That's not true. I miss my boys, but I don't have the ex's money, and I'll never win against him.

I honestly don't care about the ex anymore, but I miss my boys.

I have two cats, but I really enjoyed watching Jello.

Maybe I'll get a dog.

Funny how one perfectly sane and rational idea causes me to do something I never in my life thought I would do.

———

Join Jessie's list and be the first to know about new releases and sales on her books!

Read Me and the Tidy Tornado, the next book in the Good Grief, Idaho series where Tammy and Justin find out that opposites really do attract. Keep reading for a sneak peek now.

sneak peek of me and the tidy tornado

Tammy

I should have bought a dog.

I stare at the large, masculine building housing the ATV dealership twenty minutes outside of my hometown of Good Grief, Idaho.

I don't know what I'm even doing here. I must have lost what little mind I had left after my marriage dissolved.

My ex liked to play mind games, only he never played by the rules.

Are there even rules for mind games?

Regardless, I'm a stickler for rules.

I never color outside the lines.

Except I'm standing in front of Foursquare ATV Sales and Service, and I'm definitely making a big loop outside the lines.

Huge.

Unheard of.

I borrowed my dad's truck.

He gave me an odd look when I asked if I could.

Of all his four daughters, I'm not exactly the one he'd expect to ask to borrow his truck.

Kori wouldn't need ask; she has her own.

It wouldn't be completely unheard of for Claire, and even Leah, who is a girly girl.

Me?

What in the world do I need a truck for?

I'm an English teacher.

My idea of a good time is hanging out at my sister's house, correcting papers while the hubbub of her and her two children flow around me.

Because my home is too quiet now that my husband left and took my boys with him.

Talk about having your heart broke.

I mentioned I was an English teacher. And yes, I know the grammar is incorrect in that last line.

That's why I decided to get a dog. Because I stopped caring.

What does it matter if I speak correctly?

It seems to be a stumbling block to people because they see me as straightlaced, serious, a stick-in-the-mud, no fun.

At least, that's what my ex said.

I straighten my purse over my shoulder, run my hand down my carefully pressed slacks, and wonder if maybe I should have changed out of my two-inch heels before I stopped at the store.

I hadn't even thought about it.

The wind ruffles my blouse as I hesitate for just a moment before deciding it doesn't matter what I wear.

People aren't going to be judging me for my clothes, and even if they do, there's nothing wrong with my outfit.

I look okay, I think.

But then, I lost twenty pounds after my husband left. I'm straight as a stick.

It wasn't the diet plan I would have chosen, but I don't regret the twenty pounds, and I suppose I could say good riddance to my ex too.

I just miss my boys.

My stomach churns.

I don't know why I'm nervous. It's not like I've never bought anything before.

I'm not going to finance it. I have plenty of money in the bank, and I'm going to write out a check.

There is nothing to be nervous about.

I walk in, and heat blows down as I pass through the doorway. The smell of oil and grease and garage hits me. Unfamiliar but not pleasant, and I wrinkle my nose.

You'd think they'd put some air fresheners or something in here.

I catch a whiff of cigarette smoke as well. I don't plan on being here long enough to worry about secondhand smoke. But I'll have to have my clothes dry-cleaned, because I can hardly show up in my English classroom reeking of cigarette smoke and garage smell. I probably ought to plan on sending my purse as well.

Maybe that is part of my problem. Maybe it doesn't matter what I smell like. Maybe it's not as bad as I think.

No. I will not listen to that voice. It's becoming louder in my head, and I absolutely am not interested in doing anything that my ex said I should.

There are what seems like dozens of four-wheelers sitting on the spacious floor. But no people in sight. The place looks deserted. Isn't there anyone here?

I'm getting ready to take a step toward the ATVs on display when something zips by my feet. I almost fall.

I think at first it is a dog, or maybe the Lord is sending me a sign that I need to turn around and leave the place immediately and go find someone who is selling puppies.

Any kind of puppy.

But my eyes focus, and I realize it's one of those monster truck toys.

Remote controlled.

Where is the person holding the control? I look around the store. I can see someone in the far corner, through a door—maybe that's where the garage smell is coming from—working on what looks like a motorcycle.

I don't know anything about motorcycles, but this one has a low seat and high handlebars, and it sparkles like a Christmas tree, even though there are no lights on it. Whatever it is, it's fancy and looks expensive.

I don't want anything fancy, and I'm not buying a motorcycle. I am going to buy an ATV. I'm not sure I am going to drive it.

One step at a time. I take a breath. I can do this.

I step forward, and out of nowhere, the truck comes again, zipping between my legs.

I almost kick it, because I certainly am not expecting it.

I realize it's been humming around for a while, and I've been ignoring it.

I look around again. Whoever is playing with the toy will probably be in big trouble with his boss when I mention it to him.

A kid wearing a T-shirt and dirty jeans comes out from another door at the far wall, wiping his face with his hands before wiping his hands on his jeans. He's chewing like maybe I interrupted his lunch, even though it's afternoon.

The humming hasn't stopped, and he's not holding a controller, so I assume it's not him.

I stop again, waiting.

I don't recognize this kid, but that's not too surprising.

My hometown of Good Grief, Idaho, doesn't have an ATV shop, so I've driven halfway to Ravens Point, which is forty minutes away.

I don't do much business in Ravens Point, and I don't know anyone there.

My mouth is open, but I haven't said anything, when the truck that's been driving around bounces into my toe.

The words I had intended aren't what comes out.

"Take me to your supervisor," I say, my tone frosty. This is the part of me that I don't like. I don't mean to be frosty. I don't mean to be cold, and I definitely don't mean to be a straightlaced, serious witch.

Guess you know who said that.

Yes. My ex.

But it's my default mode. My protection mode. I don't smile or show happiness easily. I can't let loose. I can't goof off.

I used to be able to. My ex is wrong about that. But after he left, I knew he was right—I have a tendency to be too serious. I have a tendency to not let go, and maybe it's my teacher instincts, where I am constantly correcting children all day, telling them to behave, to pay attention, to not goof off, but I know that I have these tendencies.

I think it comes with being the oldest.

Regardless, it got worse after he left.

By design. I figure if he was going to leave me because I was too serious and straightlaced, then I want to make sure that if anyone else is ever interested in me, they understand what my personality is.

That, and cold and frosty aren't my emotions. They are the wall hiding my emotions.

I do that now because it's dangerous to allow people to see what I really feel. That's where the hurt happens.

I lift my chin as the boy stares at me with his mouth open. Apparently, not too many people walk in here and ask to see the supervisor.

I know I didn't stutter, so I wait for him to get with the program.

"Uh… I guess. You from the government?"

It's my turn to stare. What in the world would make him think that?

I don't worry the question too long in my brain. Sometimes, people just don't make sense. Especially teenage boys. This is one of those times.

"No. I need to speak with him. Immediately." He is going to get a piece of my mind over slacking employees who play with toys and run them into customers.

But I don't need to explain all of that to this kid. He just works here.

"Oh, okay. He's up there."

He points to the far wall, only up.

I turn, looking. I hadn't even noticed there is an overhang and what I assume are one-sided glass windows overlooking the store.

The kind of windows where he can see us but we can't see him.

I look both ways and don't see steps.

"How do I get there?"

The kid points over toward the door I'd noticed earlier through which I'd seen the man working on the motorcycle. The stairs run the far side of that door, tucked against the wall.

"Thank you," I say, and I pause, waiting for him to supply his name.

He doesn't.

He just says, "You're welcome." And he walks off.

I try to impart manners into the children I teach every day.

I teach English, but that doesn't mean that I can't teach manners and common courtesy along with it.

I tried to instill them in my boys, too.

That was one thing their father was very good at. Being courteous. Except when he was insulting me.

The kid scratches behind his ear as he walks away.

The truck that had stopped against my toe backs up and does circles around me.

I'm annoyed. Seriously. Someone needs to stop this.

And then I think, why don't I laugh about it?

What's it hurting?

True, it isn't hurting anything.

But it is disrespectful and demeaning. I won't put up with it.

And now, instead of buying an ATV, I march angrily across the floor, not even looking at the four-wheelers that are sitting there as I pass them, eager to tell on someone and get them in trouble.

No wonder my husband didn't like me.

I don't even like myself at this moment.

Still, this is such egregiously unacceptable behavior I have to report it.

Although, if those are really single-sided windows, he might already be able to see.

A thought strikes me that is so compelling I almost stop.

Maybe he *has* seen it. Maybe he's okay with it.

I don't stop. It couldn't possibly be true.

I adjust my purse strap again, put my hand on the railing, and climb the metal stairs, my high heels clicking on the steps and reverberating throughout the store. This is just a simple warehouse building with a concrete floor and a ceiling showing exposed metal beams and ductwork. Nothing fancy. Of course, it's an ATV outlet, so it doesn't need to be.

It just needs to appeal to…men.

Maybe the truck appeals to men too.

My ex is a marketing exec in a big firm, but this whole thing would appeal to him for sure. The smell of the garage, the plainclothes building, even the remote-control truck.

There's no sign or anything on the door when I get to the top of the stairs, and I don't know whether I should knock or just walk in.

I decide to be bold.

That's the opposite of my usual decision.

I open the door and walk into a large open room—open from one end of the building to the other.

Right in the middle of the room, halfway down, there's a desk.

There's no one behind the desk. But there is a man sitting in an office chair, his feet propped up somehow on the window, facing me, and smirking.

Somehow, it doesn't surprise me to see that he is holding a remote control.

a gift from jessie

View this code through your smart phone camera to be taken to a page where you can download a FREE ebook when you sign up to get updates from Jessie Gussman! Find out why people say, "Jessie's is the only newsletter I open and read" and "You make my day brighter. Love, love, love reading your newsletters. I don't know where you find time to write books. You are so busy living life. A true blessing." and "I know from now on that I can't be drinking my morning coffee while reading your newsletter — I laughed so hard I sprayed it out all over the table!"

Claim your free book from Jessie!

escape to more faith-filled romance series by jessie gussman!

The Complete Sweet Water, North Dakota Reading Order:

Series One: Sweet Water Ranch Western Cowboy Romance (11 book series)

Series Two: Coming Home to North Dakota (12 book series)

Series Three: Flyboys of Sweet Briar Ranch in North Dakota (13 book series)

Series Four: Sweet View Ranch Western Cowboy Romance (10 book series)

Spinoffs and More! Additional Series You'll Love:

Jessie's First Series: Sweet Haven Farm (4 book series)

Small-Town Romance: The Baxter Boys (5 book series)

Bad-Boy Sweet Romance: Richmond Rebels Sweet Romance (3 book series)

Sweet Water Spinoff: Cowboy Crossing (9 book series)

Small Town Romantic Comedy: Good Grief, Idaho (5 book series)

True Stories from Jessie's Farm: Stories from Jessie Gussman's Newsletter (3 book series)

Reader-Favorite! Sweet Beach Romance: Blueberry Beach (8 book series)

Blueberry Beach Spinoff: Strawberry Sands (10 book series)

From Strawberry Sands to: Raspberry Ridge (12 book series)

Swoonfully Jolly Holiday Stories:

Holiday Romance: Cowboy Mountain Christmas (6 book series)

Cowboy Mountain Christmas Spinoff: A Heartland Cowboy Christmas (9 book series)

New and Much Loved: Mistletoe Meadows (4 books and counting!)

Laughing Through the Snow: Christmas Tree, PA Sweet Romcoms (6 short reads)